IF THE DRESS FITS

THE ALMOST WIVES CLUB, BOOK 5

NANCY WARREN

AMBLESIDE PUBLISHING

Ambleside Publishing

CHAPTER 1

abby Brock paced back and forth across the hardwood floors of her airy design studio in Beverly Hills. The elegant gold script on everything from her letterhead to her designer labels read *Evangeline*, but inside, she'd always be Gabby Brock, the girl terrified to let down her guard even for a second, or all her success could be snatched away.

Very few people in the world knew her real identity. She had remade herself into Evangeline back in her modeling days when she had stepped as far away from Gabby and the Brocks as she could. She had slipped into her new persona as easily as her brides slid into the pieces of perfection that she now designed for their weddings.

An uncommon frown creased her forehead. Consciously, she smoothed it out. Her next birthday would be her fortieth and she had no wish to undergo cosmetic procedures before they were absolutely necessary.

She could still model if she wanted to. Calls came in frequently. But she had left the business before the humiliation of having her face advertise anti-aging products. No, Evangeline stood for youth and promise and glamour. Before she became associated with skin rejuvenating serums and hair color products to hide the gray, she had transitioned from modeling into the world of fashion. Always one to sense the perfect moment to leave the party, she'd left while she was on top and smoothly gone from wearing gorgeous clothes to designing them.

Naturally, she'd hired a competent staff to oversee all the boring parts of her business, but she'd learned to sew her own clothes when she was little more than a child in the East End of London, using an ancient sewing machine of her gran's. She'd had a sense of style even then. Building an empire on frothy, expensive lingerie and stunning wedding gowns perfectly suited her needs and personality. She'd aimed for the top of the market and succeeded wildly. Until recently.

God, she wanted a cigarette.

Her business and her celebrity reputation were both in trouble. She knew she had one vicious and mentally disturbed former seamstress to blame.

Curses! Who believed in curses? The clumsy seamstress had stabbed one of their clients during her final bridal gown fitting, causing a spot of blood to bleed through the perfect white satin of her gown. Evangeline was famous for her temper and she had certainly let it rip at the bride-stabbing seamstress. But, instead of cowering away and slinking back to her workstation the dreadful shrew had risen up, shouted back—which was unthinkable in itself—and muttered something incomprehensible in a language Gabby didn't recognize and announced she had cursed both the dress and Evangeline.

Not since her first taste of success in the modeling world had Evangeline ever been smacked down. Well, that wasn't entirely true. One man who'd always given as good as he got was Wade Davenport. Which pretty much explained why they'd never married as planned.

Once Wade had exited her life, she'd been treated with delicacy and fear. She was perfectly aware that her employees were

2

frankly terrified of her, and that suited her brilliantly. When the seamstress had cursed both her and the dress, she hadn't given such nonsense as curses a moment's thought.

Nor, she was certain, had the bride. Kate Winton-Jones was a modern professional woman. Still, the moment had brimmed with awkwardness. She'd felt bad that the bride had been subjected to such a scene, and so she had gone out of her way to be gracious, even accepting an invitation to what would have undoubtedly been a most tedious wedding between Kate Winton-Jones and her rich but dull husband-to-be, Edward Carnarvon.

So, it had come as an unpleasant shock when the bride called off the wedding. At the time Gabby had recalled the curse and felt the tiniest shiver waft over her neck.

Then, that same dress was handed on to Edward's cousin, Ashley Carnarvon.

She paced harder, her heels clacking against the hardwood like castanets. She could dance the Flamenco to the echo of her own steps. When the costly dress had been passed on to Ashley Carnarvon, she should have stepped in. She could see now, in hindsight, that was her mistake. Still trying to be gracious, perhaps yet conscious of the embarrassment of being shouted at by an underling, she had graciously allowed a gown she had designed specifically for Kate Winton-Jones to be resized for the shorter, stockier Ashley. Oh, the young woman was attractive enough, but the dress was never right. And that's when the whispers online began to appear.

Blog posts and gossip rags picked up the story of the cursed dress. She was positive the seamstress she'd fired was responsible and waited for the gossip to die down. Then Ashley, who'd been handed everything on a silver platter, from the incredible dress to a handsome and extremely eligible groom, chose instead to commit bridal suicide. She'd jumped out the window on her wedding day, leaving a perfectly lovely groom and two hundred guests waiting for her Evangeline gown to walk down the aisle.

Her suicidal jump had been out of a ground floor window, and into a sports car where a sexy screenwriter waited to whisk her away, so she wasn't hurt. Evangeline, however, was badly damaged.

The rumors grew louder, the story started getting picked up. "Always treat people as though you might one day need them for a character reference," Wade had said to her once. "You're a public figure, and public opinion is important."

Wade treated everyone like they were his good friends. He remembered the names of doormen and asked after their children, he chatted with taxi drivers and said thank you to waiters. She felt that people were paid for a service and should perform it to a high standard. As she always had.

What Wade, who had grown up in a good family and gone to prestigious schools, could never understand was that her greatest fear was being found out. The fear always lurked, just under the surface, that she, the great Evangeline, was a fraud. An invention of a frightened young girl who had dragged herself up from nothing with no more to offer than a pair of extraordinary blue eyes, good bone structure, freakish height and an iron will.

She hadn't gone to finishing school or modeling school or any school but the one of hard knocks. She'd learned by watching and practicing and being ready, always ready for her moment.

And when that moment came, when a modeling scout approached her on Bond Street, while she was wearing one of her own handmade dresses, she'd grabbed the opportunity with both hands and hung on hard ever since.

Now she felt her iron clasp slipping. Once the fashion bloggers and paparazzi got hold of the ridiculous curse story, Evangeline had been too busy shoring up her business to do anything about getting that dress out of circulation.

How could she have been such a fool?

That was when the first brides started canceling their orders. Her lips thinned in an angry line and not even thoughts of Botox or collagen fillers could make them unclamp. Ungrateful wretches. She only accepted one in four of the brides who begged her to design gowns for them. Now some of the lucky ones had canceled? Well, she made a note of every name and not one of those brides would get a second chance.

To her shame she had begun accepting brides that normally she never would have taken on as clients.

And then the unthinkable happened. Instead of being shut away in an attic somewhere, her gown was passed on a third time and before she'd recovered from the insult that yet again, her lovely creation had been passed around like a bag of cheap toffies, one of her employees forwarded an online ad featuring *her* gown, *her* creation, in an advertisement for a secondhand store! Gabby felt as though all her empire were crumbling. She felt in that moment how easily it could all slip away.

Her rage that day had been monumental. When she flung her laptop across the room and it crashed into the wall, she had a moment's deep satisfaction, wishing she could smash the curse as easily.

One thing was clear. She had to get that dress back. She sent an employee to buy the gown but the woman returned empty-handed. The young punk behind the counter of the vintage store had refused to sell her the gown, said it was bringing so much business in that they would continue to display it in their front window for at least a few more weeks.

Her gown was bringing in business to a two-bit secondhand store? Oh, no.

She had always known that, ultimately, a woman could only depend on herself.

She refused to think of what she had done as stealing. She had merely gone into the vintage store when it was busy and no sharp-eyed young man hovered. Instead, an older woman dressed as though she were off to have cocktails with Dorothy Parker was in charge of the store. She'd been more interested in talking to the customers than selling clothing. It was perfect.

Gabby had waited until the store was quite busy and then breezed in and asked to try on the dress. Even though she was quite famous, and no doubt the store's owner, Joanne West, would have recognized her from their modeling days together, Jo was nowhere to be seen. Knowing this was her best chance, Evangeline stepped into a fitting room with the gown, then pushed it into the big carrier bag she had brought specifically for the purpose. Peeping through the red velvet curtain of the fitting room, she waited until the shop attendant had her back turned. She swept back out onto Melrose Avenue again before anyone even noticed the gown was missing.

However, even though the gown was hers, her conscience bothered her. A day or two later, when the vintage store was closed, she'd slipped five thousand dollars in cash, which was the price of the gown, under the door of the shop.

Now, the dress was out of circulation and that ought to be the end of it.

She glanced over to where the dress hung in one corner of her large studio. As though it were in the naughty corner. It looked a bit sorry for itself, as it should—three brides and not a single one had worn the gorgeous gown down the aisle.

Her plan was simply to wait out this unfortunate spell, and with the gown safely in her possession, no more brides could be cursed.

However, it seemed her problems weren't over yet. Her employee had not been the only one who had recognized that dress in the advertising. One reporter in particular seemed to revel in her discomfort. Wolf Dixon. Wolf Bloody Dixon. He was a nasty weasel, paparazzi of the crawliest kind, but she was discovering firsthand that while the pen might be mightier than the sword, the Internet blog was mightier than a scud missile. Orders were dropping. Clients were canceling. And that nasty pipsqueak Dixon had the gall to call her office and request an interview.

Gabby rarely hired consultants. She was too confident in her own abilities. But this mess was getting stickier and she didn't know how to get out of it. She called Sarah Marsden, a top public relations and media consultant. Sarah had managed to get a philandering senator re-elected and a drug and booze addicted celebrity, who'd flamed out so many times he'd become standard fodder for late-night comedians, back on track. Getting the smudge polished off Evangeline's image should be a piece of cake.

Shouldn't it?

CHAPTER 2

*S*arah Marsden walked into Evangeline's studio with a purposeful stride. She looked like one of her clients; slick, refined, charming, and rehearsed.

Gabby recognized the type. She was one herself.

They sized each other up for an instant before she swept forward and held out her hand. "Sarah, it's lovely to meet you. I've heard wonderful things." She spoke in a clear, well-modulated voice that echoed with English boarding schools and the Queen's garden party. She'd spent hours watching and copying Princess Diana and royal commentators on the BBC. It would take Henry Higgins himself to detect cockney origins in her speech.

"Nice to meet you, too." Sarah shook her hand briefly, and they sat down in the conversation area by the long windows. Sarah got right down to business. "I've reviewed all the media reports—and I use the word media in the broadest possible terms—and I have to tell you, this is beyond public relations. The stories are getting tons of hits and spreading. We're looking at full on crisis management."

"Crisis management? Isn't that what you do when a restaurant gives its clients food poisoning? When people die?"

"I'm not trying to be dramatic, but your business, which is based so much on your own celebrity, is in serious jeopardy."

She sighed. She felt suddenly tired of all the effort she'd put into this great empire. "What do I do?"

"Give that interview."

"To that little weasel, Dixon?"

Sarah nodded. "He's a complete ass but he's got reach. People love his bitchy columns and you've made yourself a perfect target. You've slipped out of the limelight. Get back in it. Demonstrate your success. I want to see photographs of you at weddings beside blushing brides wearing your gowns. There are brides still wearing your dresses aren't there?"

"Of course there are," she snapped. There simply weren't as many as there should be.

"Good." She nodded briskly. Made a note. "Get me a list of upcoming weddings. We'll pick the most media-friendly and get some sympathetic journalists there."

She needed sympathetic journalists now? God, she wanted a vodka soda to go with that imaginary cigarette.

"Next. Damage control."

"Isn't that what I hired you for?" She used the tone that always made her underlings quake. Sarah merely looked at her coolly.

"I'm only as good as the information I get. And so is Dixon. Where is he getting his dirt? He seems to have an inside source."

She did not want to think of betrayal within her ranks. Maybe she had a bit of a temper, but she paid her people well and expected loyalty. "My guess is the seamstress is behind it all."

Sarah tapped her gold pen on her pad of paper. "Maybe. And that's another thing we have to do. We need to track down that seamstress. You may need to pay her off, and then have her sign a gag order."

Gabby jumped up and began to pace. "Pay the woman who is single-handedly destroying my business? And my life?"

Sarah sent her the same cool look. "You hired me for my expertise. Be smart enough to take my advice."

For a second she teetered on the brink of one of her monumental rages, but she stifled her acid comments. The woman was right. "How do you suggest I find her?"

"If she's feeding Dixon information then she's in the area. Probably still in contact with some of your current staff."

She wanted to throw something. "Have they no loyalty?"

"Maybe they meet to shoot the breeze and have no idea she's pumping them for information. I suggest you have a meeting and let your people know that all their jobs are in peril. If your company goes down because of this woman and her curse, they'll be out of work."

She hated the idea of coming across as needy. She always presented a strong front, as though she were in complete control. She'd get her right hand, Salvador, to talk to the staff.

Sarah continued. "If we need to, we'll hire an investigator. We'll track her down, pay her off and shut her up."

"It's this reporter I want to shut up."

"I'm in complete agreement. But he'll only stop when his source dries up and you appear successful again. I'll draft you speaking points. He'll try to needle you, and get you to say things you don't intend to say." The woman gave her a level look. "Your temper is famous. He's going to try to get you to blow your top. You can't let him get under your skin. Do you understand me?"

"Of course I do. I shan't let him get to me."

"Good. We'll do some practice interviews. I'll play him and I'll try everything I can do to provoke you. Just stick to the script. I'll be with you during the actual interview."

Gabby shook her head. "If he sees you there, he'll be like a shark scenting blood. No. I don't want him to know I'm frightened of him or anything he can do."

Sarah nodded briskly. "You're right, of course. If you're sure you can handle him, it's better if I stay in the background."

"Oh I can handle him all right."

She waited until Sarah had left, and then she shut her door. She dug into the bottom drawer of her priceless Chippendale desk and found the pack of Players she'd hidden. She opened the long patio doors and stood by the window smoking in jerky puffs.

SHE DRESSED CAREFULLY for her interview with the reporter, Dixon. With the help of her public relations advisor she had chosen a soft, feminine dress in a dusky rose color. There was nothing high powered or businesswoman about it. Her makeup was also done in a soft palate and her hair, her glorious trademark mane of chestnut curls, hung loose. There was nothing threatening, nothing sharp or businesslike about her clothing, her look, or even her environment. She conducted the interview in the same office where she interviewed prospective brides. Instead of sitting behind her desk, she'd been coached to sit in one of the two armchairs that were normally occupied by the client and her mother.

She desperately wanted a cigarette. Gabby had given up smoking almost ten years ago, but stress brought on powerful urges and every once in a while she succumbed.

When Wolf Dixon was ushered into her office she rose, and stepped forward gracefully. At six foot one, she was a tall woman and Wolf Dixon, she was pleased to see, barely came up to her shoulder. He did not look like a wolf, he looked like a gerbil. Covering his receding chin with one of those foolish partial beards only made him look more like a rodent. She shook his hand, knowing she'd scrub it with hot water and harsh soap the minute he was gone. She froze as a camera crew came in behind him. "What's a film crew doing here?"

"I thought you knew." His feral eyes lit up with nasty triumph. "I also string for a national entertainment show." He gave her a phony sympathetic glance. "You don't mind, do you?"

What could she say? Not only would he print even more vicious lies if she refused to be filmed, but she might lose face with the employees who had already seen the camera crew arrive. And these days, Evangeline could not afford to lose face with anyone. So, she pasted on the dazzling smile that had helped make her famous and rich. "No, of course I don't mind."

He settled in one chair, gesturing to her to take the other. As though this were his office. While minions attached lapel mics to both of them, her brain was seething. She wished she could make excuses to call her PR consultant. In fact, she wished she hadn't been quite so quick to tell Sarah Marsden she could handle this herself. Why had she not realized that Wolf Dixon would pull a fast one?

When the camera was set up he said, "Let's start with a few warm-up questions."

Oh let's.

He glanced down at a pad of paper and said, "You used to be a famous model."

"I was."

What kind of a question was that? Was he trying to paint her as a has-been?

"And on your next birthday, you'll be how old?"

She smiled at him. "Mr. Dick, I'm sure you know that a woman never tells her age."

"It's Dixon," he snarled. "And, unless you've been lying about your age all this time, you'll be forty years old on your next birthday. How does it feel, when you always made your money as a fashion model, to be turning forty."

It felt as though hot embers were embedded under her skin. In fact, she tried never to think about her advancing age. But, years of training in the fashion world had taught her never to lose face. She might lose a lot of other things. Her temper for instance, but her face was her fortune. And she didn't let a wrinkle show now as she said, "As I'm sure you know, I no longer model. Instead, I run an extremely successful wedding gown and lingerie design business."

"Right." His eyes glittered as he leered at her. "And how would you describe *very successful?*"

"I've gowned top celebrities, politician's daughters, and royalty. The Evangeline brand is world-famous. That's how I measure success. A woman's wedding day is the most special day in her life." She was quoting from the talking points that she and Sarah had gone over. She was glad of the practice because the words rolled smoothly off her tongue.

"When a woman walks down the aisle to meet the man of her dreams, wearing one of my gowns, I like to think I share a little of the magic of that special day."

"And yet," he said, "Business doesn't seem to be quite so booming these days. There are rumors flying around that your business is suffering. Brides have canceled their orders. My sources tell me that your empire is crumbling."

She put her hands in her lap hoping the camera wouldn't catch the way she fisted them, digging her professionally mani-cured fingernails into her palms. She breathed in once, as Sarah had suggested she do, so as not to let rip at this nasty little rodent. She said, because she'd also been coached not to lie, "Every business goes through cycles. But I'm very confident in our prospects. My team and I work very hard to make sure each gown is perfect." The PR consultant had also coached her to use the word team instead of employees. Load of nonsense. What were they, a sports team? They were her designs and she paid people to make them and sell them, that was all there was to it.

"Inside sources also tell me that your business, you personally, and one of your very famous wedding gowns, are *cursed*." He drew his lips around the word *cursed* as though it were a sweet he could suck on. Oh how she wanted to poke that nasty pointy nose and those beady ferret eyes. Instead, as she and Sarah had practiced, she broke into a delicious, tinkling laugh. And she had been working on that delicious, tinkling laugh for many years now. The old Gabby Brock guffawed like a horse.

She looked at him as though he were a simpleton, and let his camera crew catch that. "This is the 21st century. You don't really believe in curses, do you?" Shunting the stupid question back in his silly face.

He also laughed, it was a nasty unpleasant sound. "It doesn't matter what I believe, it matters what your customers believe. I hear there's one dress in particular, the very dress, in fact, that was cursed by a seamstress you publicly humiliated, and at least three brides tried to wear it and not one of them has made it down the aisle. What do you have to say about that?"

She would not lose her temper, she would not lose her temper. She parroted Sarah's words. "I can only design a perfect dress. I can't be responsible for the personal lives of my clients."

He abandoned any pretense of looking at his notes now. He leaned forward, like a jackal going in for the kill. "Come on, don't you think it's kind of suspicious that the very dress that was cursed has never been worn down the aisle?"

"No. I don't." They had not been able to track down the seamstress. So she had to be very careful what she said.

Her head began to ring, a warning sign that she was about to fly off the handle. She dug her fingernails into her palm once more.

Before she knew what she was about to say, words that had

not been scripted by her crisis management expert came out of her mouth. "And I can prove that dress is not cursed."

The weasel appeared startled. "You can? How?"

Before she could stop the words, they came out of her mouth. "Because I'm going to wear that dress myself. When I get married."

Oh, she had him now. He went scrambling back to his questions the way his brethren would scurry down the sewer. "You're engaged?"

She sent him her most perfect smile. "I am."

"Any clues on who the lucky man might be? You've never been married, have you?"

"No. I've never married. But now, it's time."

"And who are you planning to marry?"

"Why, the love of my life of course." She mentioned the first person who came to mind. "Wade Davenport."

CHAPTER 3

$\mathcal{W}$ade Davenport sat in his office, contemplating the complexities of a proposed merger between one of his telecom companies and a rival outfit. Since he didn't much like the idea of merging, he suspected he'd buy the rivals out, which might be their plan in suggesting the deal. When his private phone rang, he glanced up in surprise. Very few people had the number, so he stopped what he was doing and checked the call display.

His eyebrows rose. Gabby? He hadn't heard from her in more than a year. The usual mix of eagerness and disgust at his own foolishness pulled at him. For a moment he contemplated not answering the call, but he'd never ever been able to resist the woman who had turned him inside out and then abandoned him. He wasn't going to do it now. "Gabby," he said when he took the call. "What a surprise."

"Hello, darling, how are you?" Her voice was like an evocative perfume, it teased a man's senses and once he'd experienced that headiness he could never forget it.

"I have a feeling it depends on what you're about to tell me." He knew that tone; it was half wheedling, half apologetic.

She laughed softly. "No one knows me like you do."

That, unfortunately, was true. He'd known Gabby Brock for a very long time. He didn't answer and so she continued after a moment. She said, "Wade, I've done a rather foolish thing."

If he wrote a list of the foolish things that woman had done it would wrap around the Earth about three times. "Could you be more specific?"

"I'm afraid it involves you."

"Now, that is a surprise. What exactly have you done?"

"Oh, Wade. It's such a long story."

"I've always found the best place to start a long story is at the beginning." The beginning, for him, had been the moment he'd caught the uncertainty in those sapphire blue eyes. She'd been a hired model at some tedious fundraiser. Hired to wear some designer's gowns and to mingle with the guests, bringing a touch of glamour to a very dull evening.

She'd been nineteen. He'd recognized the fear in the toss of the head bravado she used to cover up her nerves. He'd been drawn to her from that moment. Moth to a flame? More like an iron filing to a super-magnet.

Once again that soft laugh. "The beginning. I think my story begins so long ago that almost no one alive knows all of it but you. I think you know even parts that I've forgotten."

"Are you asking me to ghost write your autobiography?" He said it sarcastically. You could never tell with Gabby.

"Of course not. But, if my life was a book, I would have to say I was opening a new chapter."

"You've got news, haven't you?" Even though they hadn't been close for a long time, he knew she would tell him if something big were afoot. He had an awful feeling he knew what her news was and he braced himself to hear it.

She said, "Wade, darling. I've decided to get married."

He closed his eyes briefly. Even though this was exactly the news he had expected, it was as though someone had dragged him into a frigid lake and was holding him under. He couldn't seem to breathe, or move, and his limbs were starting to stiffen.

He managed to say, "Congratulations. Who's the lucky man?"

"Well, this is where it gets slightly complicated."

"What exactly is complicated about marriage?" And then he thought about it. "Oh, Gabby, he's not already married is he?"

She sounded genuinely horrified when she said, "Of course not. Whatever do you think of me?"

He couldn't possibly tell her all the things he thought about her. If the groom wasn't married, there had to be something else wrong with him for her to talk about complications. "Does he run some sort of dictatorship?"

"Really, Wade."

Now that the shock had worn off a little, he was starting to enjoy himself. She'd called *him*, hadn't she? "Is he, perhaps, in prison?"

"No. That's not the problem."

"He's engaged in some sort of nefarious trade? Lucrative but illegal?"

She began to chuckle. "Stop it."

"I know, he's royal, and you being a commoner is the stumbling block."

"Any prince would be lucky to have me," she snapped. God, he missed her.

"Well, when a woman as famously anti-marriage as you decides to get married, there has to be something very special about the gentleman in question."

"Oh, Wade. To be perfectly honest with you, I was trapped into announcing my engagement."

A truly shocking thought crossed his mind. "You're not pregnant?"

"Of course not. I see you don't follow the LA gossip blogs."

"I barely have time to read the Wall Street Journal."

"It would be easier if you knew what was going on." She let out a huge sigh. "The truth is, I've been cursed."

He shook his head. "I think this line is bad. It sounded like you said you'd been cursed."

"There's nothing wrong with the line. I have been cursed."

She'd always been so careful about what went into her body, even as she'd craved things like chocolate and tobacco that were bad for her. But he hadn't seen her in a while, maybe things had changed. Very gently, he said, "Have you been drinking?"

"No! It's true. This horrible seamstress put a curse on me and one of my wedding dresses. Right in front of the bride."

He rolled his eyes. This woman should really not employ staff. "What did you do?"

"Nothing. Honestly. It was entirely her own fault. The foolish woman stabbed my client with a pin and got blood on a brand-new dress. Naturally, I lost my temper."

He could read between the lines. "Let me guess, you screamed at her in front of the client, and said a lot of things you probably didn't mean."

"Oh no. I meant every one of them. And, if I had known what she would do, I would have added a number of other things."

"And she cursed you."

"She did. I think she might be a Gypsy. Anyway, she shouted in some other language, and then pointed a horrible bony finger at me and announced that she had cursed the dress, cursed me, and cursed my business." A slight waver in her tone was the only thing that stopped him from laughing.

"Gabby, surely you don't believe in something as foolish as a curse?"

"I didn't. Until three brides attempted to wear that beautiful gown and not a single one of them got married in it. Nasty rumors have been circulating and this poisonous reporter has been making snide insinuations and spreading evil stories about me, and now my business is suffering. Honestly, I feel like I *am* cursed."

He came back to the reason she'd called him. "You can't be very cursed if you've finally found a man you want to marry."

The pause was so long he thought the call had dropped. Finally, she said, "Well, that's a rather amusing story. You see, this horrid reporter backed me into a corner and, well, before I knew what I was doing, I told him I was getting married. And that I was wearing that wretched dress myself down the aisle. And, when he asked who I was marrying, the only name I could think of was yours."

His phone slipped out of his nerveless grasp and hit the floor with a thud. He stared down at it. He heard Gabby's voice coming from far away. For many seconds he stared down at that phone, stunned, and then gingerly reached down and picked it up again.

"Wade?" she asked sharply. "Wade?"

"Let me make absolutely certain that I heard you correctly. Did you say that you announced in some public forum that you and I are getting married?"

"I did. Is that a problem for you?"

"Not for me, precisely, it might come as somewhat of a shock to the woman I'm dating."

"Oh, Wade, you're not. Well, you'll simply have to ditch her. I need you."

He passed over how self-involved she sounded and got to the heart of the matter. "Are you seriously suggesting that you and I get married?"

"Of course not," she snapped. "You and I were disastrous together."

He smiled a little in memory. The time he'd spent with Gabby were two of the most amazing years of his life, but they hadn't been able to make it work. He sometimes thought, with Gabby, that love wasn't enough. She had always seemed so frightened that she didn't deserve love that she made it true. But, he wasn't a psychiatrist, only a man who'd loved her and been crushed. "So, what are you suggesting?"

"Well, obviously, you'll have to tell your lady friend to take a sabbatical. It would be lovely if you could come out here and be seen with me in public a few times. Just until this nonsense dies down. We're trying to track down the horrible Gypsy woman. My damage control consultants say I have to pay her some obscenely large sum of money, and get her to sign a nondisclosure agreement. Anything to shut her up. Once that's done, the story dies down, and no one will even notice that we didn't get married."

"And why exactly would I do this?"

There was a pause. Even she must realize she was asking a lot. Finally, she answered softly. "Because you loved me once. And I loved you."

He supposed there were worse reasons to turn yourself inside out.

"So? Will you do it? Please, darling."

A sane man would say no. A sane man would issue his own press release distancing himself as far as possible from the temperamental Evangeline. Wade's problem was that it was Gabby, and those two amazing years they had spent together. He said, "I'll see what I can do."

She'd known him as long as he'd known her, of course, so she knew he was saying yes to her outrageous proposal. "Oh, thank you, darling. I knew I could count on you."

When they hung up, he sat for a moment, staring at the phone. Finally, he shook his head. "Oh, you poor sap."

CHAPTER 4

*G*abby had been avoiding taking her damage control consultant's phone call. Which was ridiculous, since she was paying the woman a huge amount of money, but she knew she'd flubbed the interview with Dixon terribly and the last thing she wanted was to hear about it from a professional.

However, when Salvador announced that Sarah was at reception and would like to speak to her, she knew she had to face the woman. "Bring her to my office."

Sarah strode into the room in a superbly cut cream-colored suit. Her first words were, "What were you thinking?"

Gabby rose from behind her desk and stepped forward. "I didn't lose my temper. That was the most important thing, remember? That's what you told me. No matter what I did, I wasn't to lose my temper. That weasel Dixon kept insinuating that the curse had ruined me. I could feel my temper coming on and then suddenly, I knew what I had to do."

Sarah pulled out the speaking notes they'd practiced and peered at them. "Where does it say in your speaking notes you are to announce your engagement?"

"I was winging it," she said lamely.

The woman shook her head. "No. I gave you fall back quotations. To field a difficult question, all you had to do was deflect it with generic feel-good answers about how love conquers all, and how happy your brides are."

"But you weren't there. You don't know what it was like."

"Of course I know what it was like. This is my job. I offered to be there with you, and you refused."

Gabby was honest enough to admit her consultant was right. She sighed. "I was so certain I could handle him on my own. He threw me right from the start when he brought a camera crew."

"I know. I've seen the footage." Sarah was pacing. "You should've called me the minute you saw the cameras."

"I thought about it, but I did not want to lose face in front of my staff. He keeps quoting 'inside sources' and I have to assume that someone's being disloyal. The last thing I want is for my staff to see me running scared. I am the captain of this ship. If it goes down we all go down together."

Sarah shook her head. "No. You are a team. Anytime anyone in the media asks you about your employees, you do not say you are the captain of a ship. You rhapsodize about your team. You could not do it without them. Every person on your staff is an artist or professional. Do we have to go over this again?"

"No." She slumped into the very chair she'd sat in when Dixon interviewed her. "Is it very terrible?"

Sarah seesawed her hand back and forth as though she couldn't make up her mind whether it was terrible or not so terrible. Evangeline, trying to be an optimist, decided to take that as a *not so bad*. She said, "Before you ask, I have spoken to Wade. He completely understands my predicament and is flying out to be by my side, pose for some engagement pictures and give a few selected media interviews."

The woman nodded briskly. "Good. That's an excellent first

step." She pulled out a tablet computer, opened a file and began to make some notes. "Have you got your engagement ring?"

"Engagement ring?"

Sarah seemed to resist rolling her eyes with an effort. "People will be looking for the ring. It's one of those symbols that makes an engagement seem real." She shook her finger at Evangeline. "And you need to do everything you can to make this seem real."

"All right. I'll get a ring."

"Don't you dare buy it yourself. We live in a point-and-shoot world. Someone will see you, upload the image or sell it to Dixon and your plot will backfire—" she snapped her fingers "—like that."

"Well I can't ask Wade to buy an engagement ring. Especially when I have no intention of marrying him."

"Give him the money, and make sure he's very visible when he buys the ring. We absolutely want somebody in Tiffany's following a hot tip. He's to mention your name."

If she'd ever married, Gabby had always intended to do it quietly, out of the media spotlight. "It's all so humiliating."

"If you want to dig yourself out of this mess and get your business back, you'll take a little humiliation."

"For someone who's supposedly a public relations expert you're not very nice."

"I don't have to be nice to the client; we have to present a good face to the public. Which means you do everything you can to look like a happily engaged woman."

"All right, the ring. What else do I have to do?"

"Wear that dress."

She wrinkled her nose. "Four brides have handled that dress, I'm not putting it on."

Sarah nodded vigorously. "Oh yes you are. We are going to release photographs of you trying on the wedding gown and you looking deliriously happy."

"All right, anything else?"

Sarah scanned her notes. "Oh yes. Engagement party."

Her eyes flew open. "What?"

"The party to celebrate your engagement. You will invite influential people, former clients, and selected members of the media. Remember, you are still a recognizable public figure. A celebrity in your own right. People are fascinated by you. Make the most of it."

Gabby stared at the dress still hanging in her office. For some reason, she had left it there. "That dress will never fit me. I'll have the staff make me an identical one."

"And have your inside source whisper to that reporter that you're too frightened to wear the cursed dress? Do you really think that's going to look good in the media?"

She scowled. "I'm beginning to hate you. You're too much like me. Anything else?" She really wanted this woman out of her office so she could sneak onto her balcony and smoke one of her hidden cigarettes.

"You still need to get hold of the woman who cursed you."

"I thought you were doing that."

"We haven't had any luck tracking her down. You're going to have to hire an investigator. A discreet one. I can give you some names."

"But I gave you her last address."

"I know. I went over myself, but the woman who answered the door says your former seamstress has moved out. She may have returned to eastern Europe."

"Well good riddance to her."

"Except that all she needs is an Internet connection and she can continue making trouble for you."

"Oh, how did I ever get into such a mess?" She rubbed her temples.

The woman didn't answer her. She said briskly, "This isn't a disaster. So long as you and your new fiancé act completely in love you'll brush through this thing okay. You must be very devoted to your business to be willing to get married for it."

Her head jerked up at that. "Married? Of course I'm not getting married. No, Wade and I will pretend we're getting married and then when the gossip dies down, we'll go our separate ways."

Sarah drilled her with a cold glance. "Which will make you the fourth bride who doesn't get married in that dress."

She felt extremely irked at her media relations expert. "You expect me to marry a man I don't love?"

"I didn't put you into this mess. I didn't tell you to announce your engagement. Don't ask me to get you out of it."

Which seemed completely unfair to Gabby. That's exactly what she expected from a damage control expert.

After Sarah left her office Gabby tried to work on one of the gowns that she still had a commission for. The usual magic simply wasn't with her. Unlike many celebrity designers, she actually designed her own gowns. It was a talent she'd discovered young and her years in the fashion industry had sharpened her abilities.

She had tried to avoid reading any articles about herself and her business but all of a sudden she felt that she needed to know the worst. She ditched her design pad and pressed the intercom that would put her through to her assistant. "Salvador? I need you to bring me everything you can find on this wretched curse." There was no point pretending he and every one of her staff didn't know all about the curse. He said, "Are you sure you want to read it all?"

Oh great, it was that bad. "Yes. I do."

He didn't take long to appear with a bulging file folder. "I printed out most of the Internet stories and I'll send you the TV links." She'd already seen the one on the biggest national entertainment show. The clip had made a joke about the curse, and a much bigger deal about the legendary bachelorette finally marrying her former love. Barf. But there were more of them?

"Thank you." She glanced up at him as he was leaving. "And I don't want to be disturbed."

It was one thing to stop that curse and quite another to read about herself and her problems on popular blogs and media. Even though these were the lowest gossip rags and websites, she knew how influential they could be and somehow, she supposed because of her high profile as a media darling, the gossipy stories had risen out of the gutter and become mainstream.

When she finished reading all the articles and blog posts, she sat back. Her fingers itched for a cigarette.

She called her PR consultant. "I want to issue a press release, formally announcing my engagement."

"It's already drafted. But you'd better get a ring, we want a photo with both you and the ring."

"All right."

Wade texted her: "Arriving LAX 2 PM tomorrow."

Even though she felt somewhat guilty that she'd dragged him to the other side of the country for such an enormous favor, she also had a comfortable feeling when he was by her side, like everything would be all right. She texted back, "I'll meet you at the airport."

He texted back, "photo op?"

She supposed she deserved that, but in truth she wanted to rest her head on his broad shoulder. There were so few men in the world whose shoulder she could rest her head on. Wade, at a commanding six foot five, made her feel tiny, delicate. She stood head and shoulders above most people, especially in her heels. Usually she enjoyed the feeling, but sometimes it was a pleasure to feel delicate.

She dressed with care the next day and when Wade stepped out into the arrivals lounge she felt a rush of confused emotions. He caught sight of her and shook his head, and then broke into a broad grin.

She ran forward and threw her arms around him. "Thank you for coming."

He must have heard the cameras at the same moment she did for he pulled her closer, lifted her chin up and kissed her.

For a moment she was taken back to the beginning. To the first time they met and all the years between. When he kissed her, she was nineteen again, tasting her first success in modeling and scared to death most of the time. Wade had understood her and believed in her when she neither understood nor believed in herself.

He pulled away slowly and she felt breathless.

"Well," she said. "We've got a full day planned."

"We do?"

"Absolutely. Darling, I'm very sorry about this, but we have to go and buy an engagement ring."

He burst out laughing. He simply stopped dead in the middle of the airport and laughed so hard he had to bend down and support his hands on his knees.

"What is so funny?" She hadn't forgotten, if he had, that they were under media scrutiny. When he stood his eyes were still dancing. "How many times did I ask you to marry me? You have to admit, there's a certain poetic justice to you asking me."

"I didn't ask you." She'd announced it instead, which wasn't a great deal better.

"You were completely desperate. Admit it. I saved you from yourself, again."

She put her straight, classical nose in the air. "A gentleman wouldn't remind me."

"A gentleman would bore you within five minutes."

It was true.

They walked out to where her driver was waiting. In true, Wade fashion, he said, "Hi, I'm Wade."

"Carlos." He took Wade's single bag and put it in the trunk of the town car. Wade opened the car door for her and they settled inside.

She glanced over at him. He looked good. As though he had known he would be under scrutiny, he was wearing a blue suit. "You look as though you're about to go into a top-level business meeting." She felt an unfamiliar stab of remorse. "I'm so sorry to drag you away."

"It's all right. I do have business here. The trip's not a complete waste."

She felt some relief at that even as she bristled slightly that spending time with her might be considered a complete waste by a man who had once adored her. "Honestly, I'll pay you back for the ring. But you'll have to appear to be the one who buys it."

His eyes brimmed with teasing humor. "It *would* look suspicious if you bought your own engagement ring."

She jabbed him with her elbow.

He leaned forward and said to the driver, "Carlos, can you take us to Harry Winston, please, in Beverly Hills."

Even though she was secretly impressed she said, "Darling, you know you have to make an appointment."

"I called when I got off the plane. They're expecting us."

His high-handedness annoyed her and yet there was something oddly nice after these months of torment and feeling so alone to have Wade at her side. Even though it was a charade, he still felt like someone she could depend on. The only friend she had been able to think of when trouble hit fast and hard.

Besides, it was hard to argue with a man who whisked a girl to Harry Winston.

CHAPTER 5

*H*er driver pulled up in front of Harry Winston and soon they were ushered inside. Wade took charge and she was rather happy to let him.

"Mr. Davenport, it's a pleasure to meet you. My name is Martin Bonnycastle."

They shook hands. Wade said, "Allow me to introduce my fiancée, Evangeline." He always said that was her stage name and never used it if he could help it. She appreciated him remembering how important it was at this moment that every word and deed go toward a positive image for Evangeline, businesswoman and brand.

"It's an honor to meet you," Martin Bonnycastle said with exactly the right amount of deference. They had celebrities in here all the time so she doubted he was wildly impressed, but he gave the impression that only good manners and training stopped him from gushing.

They were led to a comfortable seating area and she was shown a selection of rings. It was very clear that there had already been some discussion between Wade and Martin. There was a choice of settings but each of the center stones had to be several carats. While she considered settings, Wade paid more attention to the actual quality of the diamond. He had always been a stickler for quality. Even though this was only pretend, there was something delicious about trying on engagement rings. Oh, she'd done that a few times, but never actually got through an engagement.

So, to see an exceptional diamond in a stunning setting glittering from her ring finger gave her a sentimental moment. She felt that she was sharing in the magic that she always provided for her brides. Of course, she was rather like the tiny man behind the curtain in the Wizard of Oz. She knew there really was no magic. It was all brilliant glittery diamonds and fabric draped to hide figure flaws.

It was fun playing pretend as she tried on ring after ring, considering various styles. She and Wade both agreed on a classic cushion-cut diamond. The band was platinum and a ring of small but perfect diamonds surrounded the large center stone. The obliging Martin also demonstrated how the engagement ring and the wedding band would fit together perfectly. The price was substantial, and, knowing that for publicity's sake, she would not be able to use her credit card, she began to look for something smaller. Wade stopped her. He said, "Don't take that one off. It's the one. It's perfect."

There wasn't much she could say in front of staff, any one of whom could call that nasty Mr. Dixon. So, she gave him her dazzling smile then leaned forward and kissed him softly on the lips. "Thank you, darling, I absolutely love it." She had never been more sincere. She absolutely did love this dazzling and very sizable rock on her hand.

As discreetly as anything, the financial transaction took place while she moved her hand this way and that enjoying the play of light in the diamond. When they left the jewelry store Wade took her hand in his, squeezing in warning before she broke into speech about paying him back. Just as well because the second they hit the street someone started snapping photos of them. "Damn paparazzi," she said furiously.

"Smile, darling. This one's tame. I called him myself."

"You did what?" She said between gritted teeth. He laughed and put an arm around her, pulling her close. "Haven't you ever heard that the best defense is a good offense? This way, your Mr. Dixon will be the last one to get the news."

Her irritation turned to amusement. "I like the way you think."

"Let's give them something to write about," he said, and pulled her in and kissed her, a real one this time. While life went on around them, she had the strangest feeling that time had stopped, as though there were only the two of them.

She was breathless when the snap-happy photographer, blogger, photojournalist, whatever he was, ran up and said, "Wow. Let's see the rock."

Obligingly she flashed the diamond while the young photographer snapped more photos. "You're really getting married? Finally?" the reporter asked her.

"Yes, finally. It's time." She glanced at Wade from under her lashes. "When he called me and begged me, I finally gave in."

"He's asked you before?"

She giggled girlishly. "Oh, yes."

He turned to Wade, standing stiffly beside her. "How many times did you propose?"

He sighed. "Probably ten." The irony was that while she'd lied about him calling to beg her to marry him, he was telling the truth.

"And what made you say yes this time?"

"He finally wore down my resistance."

And then her Town Car rolled up beside them. They slipped in and before the door slammed shut, the young reporter yelled, "Good luck."

They eased back into traffic. And there they sat. In traffic.

Not all the money or all the influence could change the traffic patterns of LA. She could not stop staring at the diamond on her wedding ring finger. "This ring cost a fortune. What if they won't take it back?"

He patted her hand. "Then you can consider it a gift from me to you."

She wrinkled her nose. "What would I do with an engagement ring if I didn't get married?"

"You'll think of something."

She couldn't imagine having her ring refashioned into another piece of jewelry. It would always be a reminder of the time Wade had bailed her out of a jam and spent a great deal of money doing so. It didn't seem quite right.

But she knew that if she insisted on paying him back they'd only get into one of their silly arguments. It wasn't that he couldn't afford this ring and many more—he'd become very wealthy during the time she'd known him, rising as an investment banker to become an entrepreneur. Now he bought entire companies that were struggling and put them back on their feet. Some he sold, some he kept.

With no reporters in the immediate vicinity they both settled into their own corners of the town car. He said, "I hope you don't mind, Gabby, but I do have a meeting."

"Of course, we'll drop you. What time do you want Carlos to pick you up and bring you back to my place."

"Your place?" He shook his head. "I'm staying downtown at a hotel."

"But that's ridiculous. We're supposed to be engaged. How will it look if you put up at a hotel?"

"Like I'm an old-fashioned guy."

She pouted but he took no notice so she soon abandoned the effort. "Well, if you won't stay at my house, we should at least try and be seen together a few places. I bought tickets to a charity ball for tomorrow night. I wasn't planning to go, I only buy the tickets to support a good cause, but I wonder if we should?"

"Good thing I remembered to pack my black tie."

She was very impressed with his foresight. "You did?"

He chuckled. "I've known you a long time, Gabby. You're always dragging me to black tie affairs."

"I can't help it. I get invited to things. And it's good for my business to be seen out and about doing glamorous things."

"Everything you do is glamorous, simply because you do it." It was a lovely compliment, and he said the words in a matter-of-fact way as though he weren't trying to flatter. Merely stating truth.

Still, she was pleased. "Thank you."

"Will you need me between now and tomorrow night?"

"I hope I'll see you before then. After all, we just got engaged!" She didn't know quite what she'd imagined when he'd agreed to her plan and promised to fly out and spend some time courting the media with her, but she'd had vague ideas of all the fun they used to have together. She'd imaged intimate dinners and dancing, maybe a few weekends away. He'd always been exciting and romantic. She'd pictured, as though there were a movie screen in her head, a romantic montage of running bare-foot on the beach, sharing an ice cream, holding hands as they strolled into the best restaurants.

She'd imagined all the fun of the engagement without the actual business of getting married.

And he was booking her into his electronic calendar. "What time tomorrow night?"

"Wade . . ." She hadn't had a lover in months and Wade was here, as gorgeous as ever, and he'd just put a very expensive diamond on her finger. She put her hand on his knee and gave him a look that suggested she was open to enjoying every minute of their engagement.

He read her mind as efficiently as ever. "What about Sandra?"

"Who is Sandra?"

"The woman I'm seeing in New York."

She shook her head. "You're not seeing anyone."

His eyes darkened to flint. "And what makes you assume that?"

"I don't assume. I know. I rang Taylor if you must know and he told me you and Sandra broke up a month ago. He said you're not seeing anyone." One of the advantages of having known Wade so long was that she also knew some of his closest friends. Taylor was a darling. Funny, charming, and as incapable of commitment as he was of keeping his mouth shut.

He let out a sigh. "I should have put a gag order on that guy."

"Wouldn't have helped. It's his weakness; he always spills the beans. One of the reasons I love him."

"Can I ask a blunt question?"

It wasn't like they had anything else to do. Traffic was crawling. "Of course. We've always been honest with each other."

"Too much so I sometimes think. Here's my question. How is a bogus engagement going to solve your business problems? If we don't get married, you'll be one more woman who didn't wear that dress."

"I know. I have a two-pronged strategy. First, we haven't set a wedding date. If anyone asks, we're getting married next year. Then, next year we postpone for some reason. Hopefully by then my business will be back to booming and everyone will have forgotten all about this ridiculous curse."

"And prong number two?"

She felt her composure slip a little. "I have to get this damn curse lifted."

She felt his concern as he stared at her. "And how do you plan to do that?"

Her fingers formed a fist around her brand-new engagement

ring and she consciously smoothed them out. She wasn't going to chip her fresh manicure because of some dreadful Gypsy woman. She said, "We hired a detective to track down the woman who put a curse on me and the dress."

"And when you find her? How will you persuade her to remove the curse?"

She shrugged the shoulders that had carried millions of dollars worth of couture over the years. "Money, of course."

A slight frown pulled his brows together. "Money won't buy everybody."

"Well, in my experience, it will convince them of a lot of things."

"What if you can't find this woman?"

"I don't know. How does one lift a curse?"

She didn't mean it is a serious question but Wade seemed to treat it as such. He pondered for a moment. "I suppose you could try a witch. Or do they only put *on* curses like the three witches in Macbeth? Seems kind of un-witchlike behavior to remove curses. Unless it was a good witch."

"How should I know? I've never been cursed before."

"What about an exorcist?"

"I'm not demonically possessed," she argued.

His lips quirked. "Anyone who's witnessed one of your tantrums might disagree."

She refused to rise to his bait. He'd witnessed a few of her famous meltdowns. Caused a few, in fact. But, unlike weaker sorts, he usually yelled right back at her.

He wrapped his fingers around her hand, which was still on his knee. "I'm sure if there are people who place curses there must be other people you can hire to remove them."

When he said that it sounded so reasonable. "You really believe in the dark arts?"

"No. I don't. But, your question suggested that the dark arts were a given. I was merely being polite."

"I never believed in curses either, but I'm beginning to." She brooded for a moment, watching the unmoving traffic. "I know what I'll do, I'll get together everyone who was in that room and we'll try and remember exactly word for word what that woman said. Then there must be someone I can hire who can reverse it. And who speaks Gypsy."

He nodded looking very serious. "Excellent plan."

"There's no need to be sarcastic," she said with dignity.

He laughed. "Cheer up. If the absolute worst comes to worst you can always go back to modeling. You're still beautiful enough."

"There was a time when you wanted to marry me."

"There was. Seems like a long time ago now, doesn't it?"

"We were so young."

"We were engaged, that one summer."

"I remember it well. You're the closest I ever came to getting married." Maybe that's why his name had leapt to her lips when she'd declared she was getting married.

When they dropped Wade off at the hotel where she assumed his meeting was, he said, "I'll see you tomorrow evening then. Shall I pick you up?"

She said, "You're really not staying at my place?"

"No. I told you. I'm staying in a hotel."

"But, you're single. And I want you to stay with me." She was a newly fake-engaged woman. She felt she had rights that were being trampled.

Then, to her shock, instead of answering her properly, he leaned forward and kissed her swiftly on the lips before getting out of the car. Her driver unloaded his luggage and the bellhop whisked it away.

Wade followed the uniformed young man into the swanky hotel. He didn't look back.

She couldn't believe it. She'd actually offered to let him into her bed and he'd refused!

CHAPTER 6

*G*abby dressed with more than her usual care for the charity ball. She knew she would be under scrutiny, but she was also honest enough to admit to herself that she was dressing for Wade. He had annoyed her. Oh yes, he'd been kind enough to fly out here to help her out of this jam, but she'd always believed he cared for her deeply.

However, he was treating her now was as though she were nothing but an old friend who needed a favor. Like an irritating cousin one could never quite prevent oneself from pulling out of scrapes. Well, screw that. Wade must see her as a desirable woman who was forever out of his reach.

So, she wore a gown she'd bought from a Paris designer. It was a deep, blue silk that skimmed her body in all the right places. The designer had chosen the fabric because it exactly matched the color of her eyes. This was not a dress for fading into the corner. This was a gown that demanded attention. A bit like Gabby herself, if she was honest.

After years in the beauty business, she could do her own makeup as well or better than most of the professionals, but she did make an appointment with her hairstylist. It was a place where you had to book months in advance to get a spot but, naturally, they squeezed her in.

Wade had hired his own car and driver and, while she thought it was ridiculous when she employed her own, again she felt that shiver of approval. He was his own man and he liked control as much as she did.

When she walked into the ball, on Wade's arm, she felt the flicker of interest. Almost immediately they were approached by a fresh-faced young woman with long, straight blonde hair. She wore a chic black dress that Gabby suspected was on loan from the designer. The girl had that slick, polished look of a fashion journalist. She said, in a very posh British accent, "I'm Phoebe Baker. And you're the divine Evangeline! I'm so pleased to meet you. I'm the US editor for *Cheerio!* Magazine."

Cheerio! was a British magazine that followed the antics of the royal family and had branched out to other monarchies and, finally, to celebrities. Mostly British ones. Evangeline had of course been featured in *Cheerio!* more than once, but not since Phoebe Baker had become the editor. "How nice to meet you."

"I won't waste your time. I'd love to do a photo shoot with you and your fiancé. If we could do something with you in the next couple of days we could put it first on our online edition and then it would hit the print edition next week. How does that sound?"

It sounded fantastic. Exactly the kind of decent exposure in a well-regarded publication that would put Mr. Dixon and his slime rag to shame. But, of course, she'd been a media celebrity for too long to sound eager. She said, "That's a lovely idea. Wade and I would be delighted to appear in *Cheerio!* Call my office. My assistant will set something up."

"Of course. I look forward to it."

They circulated for a while and she quite liked the congratulations she received and the *oohs* and *aahs* over her engagement ring. Wade was the perfect date. He made sure she had a drink in her hand, he didn't cling to her side but was always ready to rescue her if she got trapped by someone boring, and he was charming to everyone. Still, deep down, she was piqued. Apart from a slightly patronizing 'you look lovely tonight,' he hadn't looked at her with hungry eyes the way he always used to.

When she'd turned instinctively to Wade, she had assumed he'd always be there for her. Oh, he was willing to help her, but his eyes didn't glow the same way when he looked at her. And he'd turned down her very clear invitation to share her bed. She wasn't sure she liked his new attitude.

After dinner and some well-meaning speeches the dancing began. Wade guided her out onto the floor and she remembered how very well they fit. Her body remembered so well the feel of being wrapped in his arms. Even his smell was familiar and very dear. After one dance he took her hand, almost abruptly, and led her back off the floor. She was positive he had felt the memory of their bodies together too and didn't like it.

As they wandered back to their table, chatting here and there and stopping to receive more congratulations, she saw a man she recognized but couldn't quite place. Then, in a flash of recognition, she realized it was Edward Carnarvon, the man who was supposed to marry Kate Winton-Jones. She excused herself and walked over to where Edward stood. Beside him was a stunning redhead wearing a dress that was just a shade too tight and makeup that was just a shade too heavily applied.

This was the woman dull Edward had chosen over the classically elegant Kate Winton-Jones? That wedding gown really *was* cursed! Of course none of her thoughts showed on her face as she said, "Excuse me, you're Edward Carnarvon?"

He turned to her. She saw him run through the same mental Rolodex that she had with him and then he said, "Evangeline."

She gave a tinkle of silvery laughter. "Very good. We've never actually met, but I designed a dress for your former fiancée."

He nodded. Then he put his arm around the redhead. "I don't believe you've met Marlene?"

They exchanged a few pleasantries. Her plan to get everyone who had been in the room when the dress was cursed back together depended on her getting hold of Kate, but the phone number she had was no longer working. She imagined Edward must have a way to get hold of his former fiancée, but she realized she could not risk discussing the cursed dress in a crowded ballroom so she said, "There's something I'd like to discuss with you."

He seemed surprised and glanced over at the redhead. It was Marlene who said, "Why don't you come by the house tomorrow?"

Come by the house? The woman made it sound like she'd be dropping by for a neighborhood potluck. But, she realized, complete privacy was all she required. If that meant 'dropping by the house,' she supposed she'd drop. She put on a gracious smile. "That would be lovely."

"I'll give you the address. Come for coffee. Anytime after ten." She winked and rubbed her lush body against Edward's. "We'll probably sleep in."

CHAPTER 7

*N*ormally, Gabby liked driving. She loved getting behind the wheel of a fast convertible. She kept her car and driver for practical reasons. She didn't waste time parking or inching along in moving traffic when she could be in the back on her cell phone, her laptop or even playing with design ideas, which she always did with paper and pencil. When he wasn't driving her, Carlos also ran errands and made deliveries.

Still, when she had the chance, it was fun to get behind the wheel. Never one to follow the instructions of a GPS, she didn't even mind it when she got lost. It was an adventure discovering new streets and neighborhoods.

Edward Carnarvon's house was not what she would have expected of one of California's wealthiest bachelors from a distinguished family. At first she thought she was lost when she entered the quiet, suburban street of modest ranch houses. She vaguely recalled that his family had not approved of the new woman in his life. Perhaps that's why he was currently living in modest circumstances. Well, it wasn't any of her business.

She pulled up in front of the small rancher, walked up the

neatly kept path and knocked on the door. The statuesque redhead opened the door. Marlene, that was her name. Even though it was Saturday morning, Marlene, like Gabby, was fully made up for the day. "Come on in. I've got the coffee on."

"Wonderful."

The house might be modest on the outside but inside someone had dropped a fair bit of money. The floors were Brazilian Cherry and the kitchen would have looked right at home in a New York penthouse. Edward was loading the dishwasher with the look of a man playing house. She said, "Good morning, Edward."

"Morning. And it's Ted."

"Thank you for seeing me today." She had rehearsed and thought about what she was going to say but there was no easy way to talk about this. She offered a few compliments on the house and Marlene told her a little bit about the area, none of which she listened to. She accepted a cup of coffee and refused the plate of cookies Marlene offered her.

When the three of them were seated in a comfortable den off the kitchen, she asked, "May we talk in complete confidence?"

Edward Carnarvon she wasn't worried about. But Red here looked like she might be the type to run to the paparazzi with tidbits of news and juicy gossip. But, as she made eye contact with Marlene, the woman's eyes began to dance with amusement. And understanding. She had a moment where she felt that she knew this woman. Had Gabby Brock not been scouted by a top modeling agency, she could imagine that she might have turned out something like this. And, she had to say, Marlene had done pretty well for herself. Ted might not be the most exciting man on the block, but he was quite a catch. Marlene said, "We'll keep our mouths shut."

It wasn't a signed nondisclosure statement but her gut said she could trust Marlene and Ted and when she listened to her gut she rarely went wrong. She nodded briskly. "I'm here because of this curse that is ruining my business. I'm sure I don't have to tell you the story behind it."

Ted drummed his blunt fingertips on his lap. A heavy gold signet ring glowed. "You don't seriously believe you've been cursed, do you?"

How to answer this? "I did not believe it when it first happened. But, in the last few months, since that crazy woman first cursed me and that dress, nothing's gone right. Not one single bride has worn that dress and it keeps getting handed on. Somebody's leaking damaging rumors to the press. All I know is my business really is suffering. If that's not a curse, then what is?"

She kept to herself the fact that the one man in all the world she had always believed would love her forever seemed to have changed his mind.

Ted said, "All of those things could simply be coincidence."

He was obviously a man who dealt with the facts and figures of the business world. He was clearly not a person of imagination. The only interesting thing he'd ever done was to take up with Marlene. Marlene, however, appeared both sympathetic and concerned. She said, "What can we do to help?"

Gabby so rarely got offered help that she was momentarily taken aback. No one in her experience helped people without expecting something in return. Then she noticed the golf-ball sized chunk of diamond on the woman's engagement finger and realized that, in fact, she did want something. Of course, this woman was getting married and she wanted Evangeline to design her a gown.

Normally, Gabby would take one look at Marlene and turn her down as a client. It wasn't that she wasn't attractive, because she was, and the statuesque body would be fun to design for. But, Evangeline dresses were part fantasy. She liked young, fresh-faced brides who were dewy with possibilities and starry-eyed with hope. Marlene had been around the block a few times and her eyes seemed less starry-eyed than cynically amused by the world.

But, Gabby knew how business worked and, the way things were going, she couldn't afford to turn down clients, not even older ones like Marlene. However, she would save that conversation until later. First, she needed to see if there was any way these two could help her. "I want your help getting hold of Kate Winton-Jones. The cell phone number I had for her no longer works."

Ted shot a glance at Marlene and then looked down at his coffee. "She had a phone on my company's plan. When the wedding didn't take place, we canceled her phone."

"Do you have a new number for her?"

Marlene said, "Why do you want to get hold of Kate? You know she's married. She's not going to wear that dress."

Gabby did know that Kate was now married, and only because the fact had been mentioned in one of the articles slagging her and her business. She said, "Yes. I do know that. I just had this idea that if I could get everyone back in the room and we tried to recreate the scene that somehow we could undo the curse." It sounded crazy. And she felt like a fool for even talking about her insane plan. Ted stared at her as though he agreed she was a crazy fool. But Marlene, again, showed an understanding. Not sympathy, which she could not have stood, but a sense of how it would feel to be in Evangeline's shoes. She said, "Why don't you ask the woman to reverse the curse? Maybe if you offered her something in return?"

"I would, but we cannot find her."

"Damn." Marlene's long, red nails fiddled with her engagement ring. "Without the person who put on the curse there is no point re-enacting the scene."

"Do you have a better idea?"

"Absolutely. I've got lots of ideas. I'm a little bit psychic you know, and very in touch with the spirit world. We'll start by doing a reading."

Ted looked as though he'd rather be playing golf. Or having his teeth drilled.

"A reading?"

"Yes. When I was an exotic dancer I learned to read Tarot cards. Settle back and try and get in touch with your inner goddess. I'll go get my deck."

She felt a headache forming. "Tarot cards? I think I need a miracle."

Marlene shrugged. "Miracles I don't do. We'll start with the cards."

She rose and went into another room, returned and handed Gabby a deck of cards that she removed from a silk bag. "I want you to shuffle the cards for as long as you like. Think about your question as you do so. Take as long as you feel you need."

Gabby shuffled the cards. They were larger than normal playing cards and felt unwieldy in her hands. She tried to tamp down her skepticism; after all, if she could believe in a curse, she might as well rely on Tarot cards to help her find her way out of this mess. She tried to form the question she wanted to ask and finally settled on, "How do I get the curse on me and my business lifted?" She really focused her attention on that question as she let the cards flip through her hands. Finally, she stopped and glanced at Marlene enquiringly.

She passed the cards back and Marlene placed them so one card was in the center surrounded by four other cards. "This is a simple five card spread," she explained as she laid them out. "Very good for answering a question." As she leaned forward, her tight top stretched over her generous breasts.

Gabby felt an odd knot of tension in her belly, which was ridiculous. These were bits of cardboard with fancy pictures on them. Still, she felt a moment of fear before Marlene flipped over the card in the center.

"This represents the now, the central theme," Marlene said. "The Queen of Cups is a very good card. It indicates female energy, often a real woman who is truly there to help you. Can you think of anyone like that?"

"All I can think of is that terrible woman cursing me."

"This woman has hair on the lighter end of the spectrum."

"Well, the seamstress who cursed me had dark hair." She ran through the blondes she knew but couldn't think of anyone who could be a positive influence on her current predicament. There was her PR rep, but she paid good money for her positive influence. "Kate Winton-Jones and Tasmine Ford are both blondes," she realized after a moment. "But they both rejected my gown and helped put me into this mess."

"The Queen of Cups is also associated with the excitement of a brand new love."

She groaned. "I haven't got time for a brand new love, now. I have enough problems." Then she realized that both Marlene and Ted were staring and that her engagement ring was flashing at her like a warning beacon. "I mean, obviously, I'm engaged to a man I've known for years. That's the only love I'm interested in." She thought it was a smooth recovery, but Marlene's gaze was strangely penetrating. What if she really was psychic?

Marlene flipped over a second card.

Gabby groaned. "The Fool. That seems about right."

Marlene touched the edge of the card with her fingernail. "The fool can actually be good. It can suggest a free and happy spirit and spontaneity. However, in your case it's reversed which suggests recklessness and, instead of a free and happy spirit, it's about unnecessary risk-taking." She glanced across the table at Gabby. "But that's your past."

"Let's hope the future is going to be better."

"That's what the next card is about." She flipped and nodded. "The Wheel of Fortune. This one reminds us things are always changing. It's a reminder to live in the moment and, even if you're on the bottom you'll always rise again to the top. In a relationship, it can mean you need to put some effort into making your relationship work."

She turned over the next card. "And here's the Sun." An enormous full sun, with a self-contented face and rays reaching down to earth beamed at her, while an exuberant figure on a white unicorn rode through.

"That's a good card, right?" It looked so happy, it had to be good.

"Part of interpreting the cards is in what you believe they mean. But I would say, yes. The sun suggests you have come out of the darkness and into the light. It literally sheds light on the situation, suggesting clarity after darkness and confusion. It suggests success, completion. This card should help shed light on your past."

Please let it be a good one. Even as she tried to remind herself not to take a pack of cards seriously, she clenched her fingers together as Marlene moved to the last card.

"And your final card, which suggests the potential within this situation." Marlene turned over the card and smiled. "Well look at that. The Lovers."

"Lovers?" How interesting, seeing that the man she was engaged to had been very clear that their relationship was strictly that of an old friend doing a big favor for another.

"Usually these cards mean what you think they mean. In the big picture, The Lovers card usually suggests finding your true love. Choosing with your heart."

Choosing with her heart. When had she last done that? She had a moment's pang of sadness.

Marlene sat back and contemplated the five upturned cards. "Wow. You have a lot of major arcana in your reading."

The cards were lovely and the costuming on some of the characters was surprisingly intricate. "What does that mean?"

"It means you're experiencing life-changing events that will have long-term consequences. You need to pay attention to what's going on in your life."

"Why do you think I'm here?" She sucked in a breath. "I think getting cursed is kind of a life-changing moment."

Marlene ran her hands in the air above the upturned cards as though reading their aura. She said, "That was in the past. This is about your future. I really find this stuff fascinating. There are so many powerful forces in our lives, some of which we don't even understand."

Gabby could only nod.

Her gaze strayed to the last card in the reading.

The Lovers.

Marlene tapped her talons against the tabletop. "What about your hair? Did she have access to your hair?"

It was such an abrupt change of subject that Gabby glanced at Ted as though he could interpret Marlene-speak, but he appeared as baffled as she was. "My hair?"

Marlene nodded. "Remember when we were in Bali, Ted? The Balinese believe you can inflict evil spirits on someone through strands of their hair. It's amazing what those evil spirits can do. This Balinese woman was telling me about how one woman cursed a rival and all her teeth fell out. Another caused his enemy to fade away and die."

"How would I get a hair devil removed?"

"Probably we'd have to bring over a Balinese witch doctor." Marlene glanced up at her. "Was your seamstress Indonesian?"

"I don't think so. I think she was Eastern European." But how well did she know any of her staff, really?

"It's something to think about."

"I'll add Balinese witch doctor to the list," she said. At least she still had her teeth.

"Maybe, since we don't know what we're dealing with, we should bring in some more consultants. I had a fantastic Feng Shui expert come through this house right after Ted moved in.

She was great. We changed bedrooms when we found out our romance corner was in the TV room. I like my TV, but, you know."

She rose to leave.

They exchanged information. She gave Marlene her personal cell phone number, something she gave to very few people. That's how much she had come to trust this woman. And, as she gathered her things ready to leave she said, "Thank you."

Marlene glanced at the Tarot reading still set out on the table and said, "Why not snap a photo of the reading? Just use your smart phone. You might want to refer back."

She did so, more to be polite than because she thought she'd spend much time poring over those five cards and their meanings. Then she put her phone away and said, "I'll save you the trouble of asking. I'd be more than happy to design your wedding gown."

She was moved by her own generosity. While she waited for Marlene and Ted to gush their thanks, to her surprise, Marlene glanced at Ted, looking alarmed. He shook his head slightly.

Finally, Marlene fiddled with the Tarot cards so she didn't meet Gabby's gaze. "Oh. Wow. That's so nice of you. But, an Evangeline gown's not for me. I'm not some blushing young rose, just opening into bud, I've been in full bloom for a while and some of my petals are starting to droop."

"I think you're fantastic, babe," Ted said loyally.

She winked at him. "Anyway, we're getting married in Vegas."

"Vegas?" Edward Carnarvon the third or fourth, or whatever number he was, planned to marry in *Vegas*?

"Sure. I'm going to wear something with a lot of sparkles. We'll gamble, we'll catch a few shows and we'll have a fantastic time."

She glanced over at Ted, expecting him to look as horrified as she felt, and saw that he was grinning in anticipation.

These two might not look like a pair but deep down they matched.

"That's wonderful. Congratulations. Well, if you change your mind, the offer stands."

"I appreciate it." Marlene said, but Gabby couldn't quite get over the feeling that Marlene was the one being generous.

She got back in her car and wondered what had just happened. She had offered Marlene her exclusive, sought after services and she'd had her generous offer thrown back in her face.

Would this curse never end?

ade found Gabby in the garden. He'd arrived more than an hour early for their *Cheerio!* interview. He had a few reasons for being so prompt. A confused housekeeper answered the door and claimed no knowledge of Evangeline's whereabouts, until he introduced himself as Wade, the fiancé. Was it his imagination or did the woman look at him with pity? He wondered how long was the line of saps to fall for Gabby's undeniable beauty. She grudgingly admitted that Miss Evangeline was in the garden.

He strolled around the side of the Bel Air mansion past the obligatory topaz of the swimming pool and there she was, kneeling in dirt, her hands in gardening gloves to protect the delicate skin and no doubt her fresh manicure, happily pulling weeds. She wore old jeans and a Yale sweatshirt he suspected had once been his. A large-brimmed hat protected her face from the sun and he thought the sight of her working methodically in the dirt was as lovely as anything he'd ever seen. He watched her for a minute or two and then, not wanting to startle her, called: "Gabby?"

She dropped her gardening fork and turned around. She rose with a smile. "I hope you're early and I'm not late."

"The interview's not for an hour. I thought it would be smart of me to come and check out the place. If I'm supposed to be marrying you I should probably know what your house looks like."

She laughed but he was certain he saw a faint blush. "My bedroom you mean."

"It crossed my mind that a man who is set to marry you should know what the inside of your bedroom looks like."

She nodded briskly. "I'll just tidy up here and take you on the tour."

When she'd finished putting her tools away, she put her hand in his arm and walked him up the path, across a flagstone patio furnished with deep and comfortable looking wicker furniture and through the patio doors and into the house. "This is the music room," she said as they entered.

"You have a music room?" There was a grand piano, a complicated looking sound system and a couple of guitars on stands.

She laughed. "I know, I can't play a note on any musical instrument. My singing voice is worse, but the house came with the music room and somehow it appealed to me. Back in the thirties, this place was owned by a Broadway star. I like to imagine old-time actors gathered around the piano, Mae West sitting on it and cracking jokes."

As she led him through the house he realized that she had possibly unconsciously re-created the home she had once dreamed of owning. He'd been in London on business back when they were in the heyday of being in love and she had squealed with joy when she saw a real estate listing for a place in the Cotswolds. In her usual, spontaneous fashion, she'd dragged him down to some tiny town with a ridiculous name like Middlebury-on-the-

Toadstool and walked him through a stone manor house that had probably sat on that very spot for half a millennium. The house had been owned by smart Londoners who'd hired a fancy decorator to create his signature brand of high style country living. That's what this home reminded him of. The English antiques, drapes and carpets, the paintings and the gilt mirrors. She'd brought the Cotswolds to California. Upstairs she showed him an enormous, sensual bathroom, three guest rooms—one of which she used as a home office—and then, last of all, her bedroom.

"It looks like something Cleopatra slept in," he said, gazing at the huge four-poster bed with a silk duvet and about a dozen lace pillows. A green velvet chaise with stubby curved legs angled across one corner of the room, large china leopards flanked a fireplace and full-length French doors opened onto a balcony that overlooked her garden. The one thing that struck him was that this woman who had been blessed with extraordinary beauty and who had made her fortune off her face had not a single mirror in her bedroom.

There were no signs of a recent gentleman caller and he didn't ask.

She took him back downstairs and said, "I'd better go and change. Juanita will make you some coffee."

She would have taken him by the hand and led him into the kitchen, but he stopped her. "I can find her. You make yourself ready."

He knew it wouldn't take her long; he'd never known a woman who could get ready so quickly. Maybe it was her background in fashion. He understood they did lightning-fast changes when they were doing runway shows.

He walked back to the kitchen and found the woman who had let him in peeling vegetables. "Juanita?"

"Yes." She stepped away from the sink and wiped her wet hands on her apron. "What can I get you, sir?"

He shook his head. "Carry on with what you're doing. I don't really want anything. I thought we'd get to know each other while Evangeline is getting ready. And please, call me Wade."

She seemed a little uncomfortable making small talk in her kitchen. She seemed to have a need to feed or water him. "Coffee? How about some water? Or some tea? I've got iced tea in the fridge? Or, if you're hungry, I could make you some eggs."

He suddenly felt foolish being in the kitchen and not eating food as though he had somehow trespassed on her territory with false intentions. He said, "Coffee. Coffee would be good."

She seemed very relieved to have something to occupy her hands and immediately bustled about making coffee. He sat at the kitchen table and asked, "How long have you been with Evangeline?"

"Going on three years now."

"were?"

The efficient hands paused for a moment and then carried on. "Yes. She did."

She made him coffee and he tried to convince her to have a cup with him but she steadfastly refused.

He glanced around and compared this place to his much smaller townhouse in Manhattan. "This is a lot of house for one person."

The housekeeper nodded. "Will be much better when there are children."

He was startled. Children? What did Juanita mean? Was she merely, in the Latin way, assuming marriage meant children? He wanted to follow up, but at that moment Gabby appeared in the kitchen doorway, looking absolutely ravishing. She'd combed her hair, done something with her lips and eyes, and wore loose silk trousers and a matching jacket in ivory silk. Her engagement ring flashed, as did the diamonds at her ears

"I see you're making friends with Juanita."

And not getting very far.

"Come on into the living room and we'll rehearse for the interview."

His eyebrows rose. "We have to rehearse?"

"I've prepared a folder for you. It's got the highlights of my life in the last few years. Background for the interview."

"Sorry, I forgot to print out my resume for you."

She ignored his sarcasm. "Not to burst your balloon, darling, but they're more interested in me."

He pretended hurt. "You mean next time I get engaged, *Cheerio!* won't want an in-depth interview?"

He'd meant it as a joke, but she turned and grabbed his arm. "You're not thinking of getting engaged, are you?"

For a second he felt as though she actually cared about him, then reason reasserted itself and he understood she was afraid that the second the curse was lifted, he'd go marry someone else and she'd have a new PR disaster on her hands. "No. I'm not."

"Oh, I'm so relieved."

He couldn't help but smile at her. "For now, I'm all yours."

She sent him an enigmatic look. "I had a Tarot card reading, you know, as part of my efforts to rid myself of this curse."

"Really? Did it work?" He tried to keep an open mind about things, but he didn't seriously believe a pack of cards with pretty pictures on them could lift a curse. But then, he didn't believe in curses either.

She shrugged. "Apparently things are going to work out in the end."

"Now that, I do believe."

When they got to the living room, she handed him a file folder. He knew all about the old Gabby but this new woman was a bit of a mystery. She settled in beside him, put her feet up on the coffee table and slipped a pillow behind her back. It was so familiar that a wave of nostalgia swept over him. How often had they sat together, talking about everything and nothing, their hopes and dreams, their separate paths and what he'd believed would be their shared future. He opened the file and began flipping through clippings, highlights of her life as told in sound bites and torn magazine pages.

A lot of the photos he recognized. There she was at the Oscars with her movie star boyfriend. Here was the opening of her design studio. She'd invited him to that event, but he'd been in Beijing on business. "I'm sorry I missed your opening."

"We had quite the party," she recalled, looking over his shoulder.

"What's this?" he asked, looking at a photograph of Gabby with four young women and a young man in front of a depressing brick building.

"Those are my scholarship students," she said, with a hint of pride.

"So, you did it then?" She'd said she wanted to provide a chance to London kids like her who'd grown up with nothing.

"Sure, but let's not bring that up. It's not relevant."

"Okay." But he was happy that Gabby had indeed fulfilled that dream. He liked that she played it down.

She shifted so she was facing him. Mimed holding a microphone. "Wade, tell me how you and Evangeline met?" She asked as though she were an interviewer. She'd been interviewed often enough that she could easily imitate the upbeat, staccato tones of a reporter.

He let his memory drift back. "I was in London. I was a young international banker. I'd just come off a trip to Hong Kong and Zurich. London was my last stop before heading back to New York.

"The firm we were affiliated with had bought a table at some big charity event with everybody who was anybody. We were doing the rounds when I glanced up and there you were. You were what, nineteen? And you looked a bit like a kid at her first grown-up party. Your eyes were big and round and you were taking it all in. You held a glass of champagne but you didn't drink. Every guy there wanted to be with you. I knew I couldn't leave without at least talking to you."

She smiled. "You were very persistent. Very American."

"You were wearing this amazing black dress and I couldn't take my eyes off you. You were all legs and there was some kind of lace panel in the chest area that drove a man crazy wondering."

She laughed. "I can't believe you remember that dress. It was on loan from a designer, but he gave it to me in the end. He said I was his muse."

"I remember the dress, but I don't even remember what we talked about. I know I tried to impress you, acting like I was such a big shot and I was all of, what, twenty-four?"

"You did impress me. You seemed wildly sophisticated to me when you talked about politics and books and music as though you knew all about them."

"I was faking it, mostly." He settled back, his hand drifted to her knee. "We talked and danced all evening and then, when the party was breaking up, I said to you—"

"Don't make me leave England without knowing you better."

He squinted his eyes in pain. "Remember, I was only twenty-four. I'd be smoother now."

"You were plenty smooth for me."

"And from that moment until five days later when I got on the plane to go back to New York, every second we weren't working, we were together."

He used to tell people that he fell in love in five days. It wasn't true. He fell in love the first second he saw her.

"Those may have been the best five days of my life."

"And then you got a modeling job in New York."

"Excuse me, I got plenty of jobs in New York." She stuck her perfect nose in the air. "I was a success."

He chuckled. "You were at that. A genuine supermodel."

"And within a year we were engaged."

"That we were."

She leaned over and put her head on his shoulder. He smelled the familiar scent of her and she said, "What happened to us, Wade?"

He shrugged and felt the silky thickness of her hair against his shoulder. "I don't know. Fame? We both got too invested in our careers?" He shot her a sideways glance. "Your temper?"

She dug an elbow into his diaphragm but softly. "You never minded my temper. In fact, I think you were the only one I never scared away." She let out a sigh. "I am impossible, aren't I?"

"Not impossible. Challenging."

There was silence for a moment. "Did I break your heart?"

She'd used a rusty cleaver, sawed through his sternum, ripped open his ribs, grabbed out the tender still-beating heart and stamped on it in her brand-new Louboutin heels. But he wasn't going to acknowledge how completely she'd eviscerated him. "I haven't been lonely if that's what you mean."

It wasn't and they both knew it.

"If I'd ever married anyone, it would've been you." Instead, within weeks of their scheduled wedding she'd left him a note on his pillow and fled back to England. It wasn't long after that she'd taken up with a pretty Brit movie star. For a while he'd believed she'd left him for a celebrity, but he'd kept up with her over the years as she jumped from man to man, and he'd begun to believe she hadn't left him for another man. She'd left because she was terrified.

He chuckled. "Same. And here we are both crusty old bachelors."

"Did you get close to marrying? After me I mean?"

"Sure I did. But the allure was never enough to make me give up my freedom."

Also, no one had ever come close to being to him what Gabby was. He glanced at her. "How about you?"

Those deep sapphire eyes connected with his. "Not really. Peter was very sweet but even more insecure than I am. And I think he wanted the limelight more. Of course, that would never do. Then I thought I was in love with a Russian. Of course he called himself a prince but he probably wasn't. He was lovely though, and very, very rich. He was devoted to me but he was much too jealous. And, other than that, nobody really." She snuggled against him. "I had forgotten how comfortable you are. And how well my head fits on your shoulder." She glanced up and the lips he had lost himself in so many times were mere inches away. "Why did you come to me, Wade?"

"Because you asked."

Their past hovered in the air between them the way the possibility of a kiss hovered and then the moment was shattered by the pealing of the doorbell.

In a second he watched Gabby retreat and the very businesslike and much less lovable Evangeline take over. She replaced the cushion to the exact spot where it had been then stood to check her reflection in the mirror over the fireplace.

Juanita answered the door but Evangeline strode out to help welcome the journalist.

Wade ditched the folder in a nearby antique chest of drawers, stood and waited as the entourage piled in. Soon the elegant room seemed full.

Phoebe walked over and shook his hand. "So glad we could do this."

She had a photographer with her and the photographer had a helper and equipment. He'd forgotten what this was like. The lights and the big umbrellas. The assistant fussed with his hair and pushed his tie a quarter-inch to the left. He wanted to smack the young woman. Finally, they were arranged. Gabby took his hand but he felt it was a calculated gesture. She held it in such a way that her brand-new engagement ring faced forward. It reminded him of the official photo ops of a royal engagement.

Phoebe placed a sleek microphone on the table in front of them and drew a notebook from a large leather bag. She was as well dressed and as perfectly made up as Gabby was; he assumed it was in order to make the celebrities feel comfortable that she dressed like one of them. He was wrong. It turned out that she wanted to get pictures of herself with the happy couple. As well as writing a feature article, she was to make their engagement the subject of her own monthly editorial.

The three of them posed and lights flashed, and cameras snapped. Then they were released and allowed to sit on the couch once more.

"Do you mind?" she asked, and then without waiting for an answer carried a gilt armchair closer.

"No, of course not," Gabby replied. "Can I offer you some coffee?"

"Oh yes. Thank you. Coffee would be great."

He didn't think either of them really wanted coffee. Gabby nearly always drank green tea. In fact, she put almost nothing toxic in her body, which was why it had always amused him that she fought a constant craving for tobacco. He wondered if she still did.

He thought the point of the coffee was the visual clue it offered to *Cheerio!* readers. Here were a couple of nice English women chatting over a cup of coffee, catching up on each other's lives. While they were fully dressed to the nines and a photographer recorded every moment.

They got comfortable and chatted for a few minutes, mostly about British celebrities living in LA, and then Juanita brought in the coffee. In British bone china cups with gold rims and what looked suspiciously like a coat of arms.

Then they settled back and the interview began in earnest.

"Remind me how you two met?" Phoebe asked as her opening interview question."

Gabby giggled, and even he had to smile. She glanced at him. "Why don't you take that one, Wade?"

He got through a much shorter version of them meeting so young and their engagement the first time. She listened, nodded and when he was finished, Phoebe pulled a folder from her bag and passed it over to them. "Look what I found."

With a quizzical expression Gabby opened the folder. For a moment he felt her utter stillness as they both stared down at a photo of the two of them he'd forgotten all about. *Cheerio!* had interviewed them when they got engaged back in the nineties. How young and hopeful he looked. How absolutely convinced that everything would turn out perfectly. And Gabby, a goddess, her sensual beauty almost breathtaking. The golden couple.

After a moment, Gabby laughed, her trained Evangeline laugh. "Oh my goodness. Where did you find this old thing?" And she put a hand to her chest. "What about the way I wore my hair back then? There was so much of it!"

"So, what's different about being engaged this time?" The reporter asked.

He got the last question, let Gabby take this one. For a moment he saw her brain race and then, once more reaching to take his hand, she said, "I think we're older and wiser. Wade and I were engaged almost twenty years ago. We were too young to realize what we had. But now, I think we know. I'll never find a love like that again and I don't want to go the rest of my life without it."

Damn, he had to hand it to her. If he didn't know she was lying through her pearly white teeth, he'd believe her story himself.

Phoebe turned to him. "And you, Wade? Do you feel that way?"

What the hell. If Gabby could lie, he could tell the truth. "I've loved this woman since the first moment I saw her. I will love her to the day I die."

"Oh, Wade," Gabby said, turning to send him a melting glance. And adding the ghost of a wink.

After that it was pretty routine. "Where will you live?"

"Why, right here, though of course we'll also keep a home in New York as Wade's business is there."

Did they plan to have children?

"I can't imagine anyone who would make a better father than Wade."

He could sense the interview winding down and then the reporter asked, "Are you really going to wear that cursed wedding dress? Won't you design a brand new dress just for you?"

He felt her stiffen beside him. Then she said, "First of all, I don't believe for a moment the dress is cursed. Frankly, it's one of the most beautiful gowns the Evangeline team has ever created. I think the reason no one wore it is that it was meant for me. So no, I will not be designing myself a new gown."

"When my predecessor first interviewed you, when you got engaged back in the nineties," she mentioned the decade as though it were a long bygone era, possibly taking place around the same time as the ice age, "Evangeline, you were an up-and-coming supermodel, but you told *Cheerio!* Magazine then that you were making your own wedding dress. Is that true?"

He supposed one of the reasons she had become a super-model was that Gabby had the ability to put forth what seemed like honest emotion at whim. She appeared both proud and a little shy as she nodded. "I did make my own dress for that wedding. I didn't have the skills I have now, of course, or the lovely fabrics at my disposal, and I certainly didn't have the couturier staff that we are so proud of at Evangeline Designs. But that dress was made with love."

"Whatever happened to it?"

She shrugged. "It was a long time ago."

"Well, it's so nice to catch up with the two of you. I hope you'll send us an invitation to your wedding. We'd love to cover it."

Before she could speak, Wade said, "I'm sorry. We're not having any media at our wedding. But, don't worry, we'll make sure to send you some great shots."

She nodded graciously. And then the crew packed up. And left. As soon as the door was shut, Gabby turned on him. "Are you crazy? You just told *Cheerio!* they can't come to our wedding."

"I know I did. I don't want my wedding to be a media circus."

She gave a shriek of frustration and threw her arms in the air. "There isn't going to be a wedding!"

"Then why the hell do you care if some fancy magazine covers it or not?"

She gestured as though she were tossing a football up to God. "Now I know why I broke up with you. You're impossible."

He shook his head. "Right back at you."

CHAPTER 9

"*N*ice job on the *Cheerio!* interview," Sarah Marsden the PR consultant said as she settled in Gabby's office for what had become a weekly meeting.

"It did turn out well, didn't it?" Gabby agreed. The online article was already posted along with some very flattering photographs of her and Wade during their interview at her home. However, Sarah was not one to let a person rest on their laurels. She had her tablet computer out as well as her notebook and pen.

"We need to go over the media list for your engagement party."

It was a good thing she already knew she wasn't marrying Wade or she'd be tempted to cancel the engagement party and the engagement. After he'd so foolishly told *Cheerio!* they weren't invited to the wedding, and she'd told him to butt out in no uncertain terms, he'd left. As far as she knew he was buried in work.

Or simply ignoring her.

Gabby wasn't used to being ignored and she didn't like it one bit. She was a center-of-attention sort of person.

She gave a cursory glance at the media list. "Yes, this looks fine."

"Good. It's going to be an amazing party. Everyone who's anyone will be there. Garry Greenstein agreed to give a toast to the happy couple." Garry Greenstein was a top comedian who'd enjoyed huge success on a sit-com he'd created about living in LA. Gabby didn't know him particularly well, but was assured he'd be funny, charming, and not controversial. "He wants to do a bit about the curse, what do you think?"

She thought for a moment. "Sure, why not? Maybe if he makes fun of it, the curse will seem like a joke."

"My thoughts exactly. I don't think we've had one 'no' on the RSVP list. One of your former bridal clients even rescheduled her C-section so she can come to the party."

"That's nice."

Sarah studied her. "Is everything all right?"

The trouble was that interview. Gabby tried not to dwell on the past, but sitting with Wade and recalling their young love had put her in a strange mood. She couldn't go back and yet she wanted to. She adored Wade and he drove her crazy at the same time. She wanted to lean on him and she wanted to push him away. She rubbed her temples where a headache was threatening. "I'll be fine. Pre-wedding jitters, that's all. Wade's not an easy man to love."

Sarah's lips twitched and she could almost hear her thoughts.

Gabby felt her own lips curving in response. "You're right. I'm not easy to love, either."

"I didn't say that."

"You didn't have to. I know I'm demanding and have high standards, but sometimes I could cheerfully hit Wade on the back of the head with a frying pan."

Sarah laughed. "I've been married for five years and I have

that impulse about once a week." She played with her tablet for a minute. "I think it's part of being in love."

In love? "Really?"

"I'll be honest with you. I had my doubts you could pull off this engagement you so recklessly announced, but then I read that article and saw the photographs." She passed the tablet over and Gabby could see she'd enlarged one of the pictures from the interview. It showed her and Wade while they'd been speaking with Phoebe. It was a candid shot. They were sitting so close they were touching. She'd said something, and then turned to him and put her hand on his knee. "Look at the way you two are staring at each other, and how comfortable you are physically. You made me believe you're in love, and they don't come more cynical than me."

She glanced up, startled. The only other person, apart from Wade, who knew this engagement was fake was Sarah. And she believed they were in love. A warm glow began in her stomach, soon doused by a cold shiver of fear. She needed to get this bloody curse lifted, then she'd worry about who was in love with whom and what they were going to do about it.

"Did you choose your gown yet?"

"Yes, a red Valentino." It was a pull-out-all-the-stops gown. A rich, true red, cut to figure-flattering perfection that swept the floor with a hint of royalty. It was the color of passion and certainly a center-of-attention kind of dress. Gabby's favorite kind. Since they were apparently doing show-and-tell this morning, she got up for her own tablet, which was on her desktop, and nearly bumped into a large potted plant. With a muttered curse she changed direction and headed for her desk.

"You've been redecorating, I see."

"Feng Shui. It seems my desk was in the romance corner. Now it's in the money corner."

"I'm glad you didn't move your client seating area."

"Luckily, it was already in the communication zone." She

could not believe she was desperate enough to remove this curse that she'd hired Marlene's Feng Shui expert. Now she kept getting disoriented in her own studio. She retrieved her tablet and showed Sarah a photo of her in the gown.

The woman nodded. "Perfect. Can you send me a copy? I'll make sure the décor complements the gown. Wade is wearing a tux, I assume?"

"Yes."

Sarah nodded briskly, made a note. "We'll get him a rose boutonniere in the same red." Then she glanced up. "Even though we've chosen media that has a broad reach and also higher standards than the Wolf Dixons of journalism, you'll still need to be on your guard."

"I know. I'll go over the talking points you made me for the Dixon interview again. I'll be fine."

"What about Wade?"

"Wade will get one talking point. Don't say anything stupid."

Sarah chuckled. "Maybe I should talk to him and give him some basic sound bites."

"Fine."

Sarah stood. "And if you two have had a tiff, you need to kiss and make up before the party. Understood?"

She felt as though she were being reprimanded by a strict teacher. She let out a huff of annoyance. "Yes."

"See you on Saturday."

She had barely settled to work when Marlene called. "How's the Feng Shui working out? Is the Ch'i flowing better?"

"I don't know how Ch'i is doing, but I bruised my shin in the family section."

"Give it time."

She could not believe she was so desperate she was willing to take advice from a six-foot tall former stripper. But, there was something about Marlene that she trusted. Like Gabby, she was a woman who had taken control of an unsatisfactory life and made it better. Marlene was honest and openhearted and she respected her.

"Okay, next step. You need to get all the brides together."

"All the brides?" If she got those girls in here, she suspected she'd want to line them up and smack them.

"Every bride that was supposed to wear that dress needs to be in the same room with the dress and you."

"And then what? We do incantations and dance naked under the full moon?"

"Well, you could try that." Marlene actually seemed to take her sarcasm seriously. "But I'd start with a smudge ceremony."

"A smudge ceremony."

"Sure. It's a native tradition. You burn a special kind of sage and use it to purify things. I do a smudge ceremony every time I move, it clears the house of old spirits. I also smudge any second hand jewelry or vintage clothing."

"And you can do this smudging business?" Marlene was a woman of many talents.

"In your case, I'd call in an expert. I have a friend. She's psychic and sort of a shaman. Her name is Leandra and she runs a fantastic crystal shop downtown. You get the brides together, and make sure you have the dress there as well. I'll get Leandra."

"And you're sure this will work?" Even though she was completely skeptical she was also desperate. If she'd come to believe in the curse, she supposed it was only logical she should believe it could be lifted.

"Oh yeah. Leandra's great. And, if the smudging doesn't work, she's got some contacts with the local coven."

"Coven? As in witches?"

"Sure. There are spells they can cast to lift curses. There's one with a broken mirror, I think, that reflects the ill will back to the person who cursed you. And there are potions you can try."

She didn't like the sound of anything involving broken

mirrors and she most certainly wasn't going to drink anything that could contain eye of newt.

"This is like a mysterious disease. You keep trying different cures until you hit on the one that works."

"You're saying my dress is like a disease?"

Marlene had a great laugh. Earthy and rich. "Not the dress, honey, the curse. The curse is like a disease. But we can't cure it until we know what kind of disease. Is this bacteria? Is it a virus? Cancer? We don't know until we keep trying treatments and we discover what works."

"It better not be cancer." She glanced at the dress, which she still kept with her. It hung in the romance section of her studio but she didn't care. She liked where it was and wasn't about to move it.

Gabby called Kate Winton-Jones first. When Gabby explained about the smudge ceremony she seemed hesitant. So, the designer laid on the guilt. After all, if Kate had gone ahead and married Ted like she was supposed to do, everything would have been fine. Luckily, she didn't have to press too hard. She could tell Kate was one of those laudable women who tried to do the right thing. Abandoning her wedding, her groom, and her designer gown, had no doubt cost her some sleep.

She agreed to make herself available and Gabby was able to check one name off her list. Since Ashley Carnarvon was Ted's cousin, he had given her updated contact information for Ashley as well. Ashley had married the up-and-coming and very sexy screenwriter Bennett Saeger. Gabby felt that Ashley, too, could have prevented the disaster if only she had worn the damned gown when she married the sexy scribbler. But, no, once again a dress most women would be thrilled to wear had been scorned. She'd passed the dress on to a bridesmaid as though it were any old thing.

Fortunately, Ashley seemed to think it would be a great lark to get together with the other brides. "This is so awesome," she said with enthusiasm. Gabby was glad that someone found this fiasco entertaining because she certainly did not. From Ashley, she got the information for Tasmine Ford who was just back from her honeymoon with Ashley's jilted groom. How nice for her. Since she didn't seem very surprised by Gabby's request, it was obvious that Ashley had already spoken to her. She didn't seem to need much convincing. Gabby got the feeling the brides found this whole thing rather amusing. She might have too if it were someone else in her predicament. As she prepared to hang up, Tasmine said, "I can put you in touch with Megan O'Reilly too."

"There's another bride?" She practically screamed the words. "Don't tell me she rejected my poor dress as well."

"Megan O'Reilly? She was saving up to buy the dress when it disappeared from the vintage store. She was heartbroken. She probably tried it on more times than any of us."

Gabby put a hand to her forehead. She could not have believed this nightmare would get worse.

"I met her when she came looking for me to see if I had taken the dress back. I was the one who took it to the vintage store in the first place." The woman's tone was slightly acidic and Gabby had to fight to keep her temper in control. Tasmine continued, "She was really upset to lose that dress. It looks amazing on her. Honestly, better than on any of us."

"How can you possibly know that?"

"I've seen her. She posed for some advertising photos. They were all over the Internet."

Gabby knew those photos well. She still wanted to grind her molars when she thought of how those ads had cheapened her brand. "The redhead?"

"Yes. The redhead. She was heartbroken when that dress was taken."

She did not like the way that young woman interpreted

71

events. She said, "I did not steal that dress. I paid full price for that gown even though I was the one who designed it."

"Well, they kept telling everyone it wasn't for sale."

"Nonsense!" she snapped. "What kind of shop owner keeps a dress in a window that's not for sale?"

"I think you should talk to her. She loved that dress and I bet her energy's all over that puppy. Anyway, here's her cell number."

Gabby wrote it down but, in fact, she already had Megan O'Reilly's contact information. Salvador had interviewed her on the phone, since he screened all potential clients. Megan O'Reilly had been very specific. She wanted to wear the gown that had recently been for sale in Joe's Past and Present vintage store.

She hadn't yet found time to return that call.

Gabby tried to convince herself she didn't need this Megan person in on the smudge ceremony since she hadn't scorned the gown. But Tasmine's words haunted her. "Her energy is all over that dress." If that were true, then Megan O'Reilly had to be included. She paced up and down her studio for a few minutes trying to work out what she would say and then, she picked up the phone.

"Megan O'Reilly," the chirpy young woman announced when she picked up her cell phone.

"Megan. My name is Evangeline. I understand you've been trying to reach me."

"Oh, wow, thanks for calling me back." She was happy to note that at least this bride sound thrilled to hear from her.

"What can I do for you?"

"Well, this is sort of awkward but I was hoping that you might consider . . ." She let out a breath. "I'm so flustered I can't even speak straight. I wore your beautiful gown for a photo shoot for Joe's Past and Present. I'm engaged and I really want to wear that dress for my wedding. Is there anything we could do to make that happen?"

She liked the edge of desperation in the young woman's tone. She hadn't heard that in far too long. A woman should be eager to wear one of her gowns.

She said, "It's strange you should call. I'm having a little get together with all the brides who were supposed to wear that particular gown. I'd be very happy if you would join us and then we can talk about how I can help you."

Tasmine Ford was right. If the redhead had modeled that gown and hoped to wear it for her wedding, she was definitely a link in the chain of misery that wrapped around Evangeline's business like the chains clanking behind Marley's ghost.

CHAPTER 10

On the night of her engagement party, Gabby had Carlos drop her at Wade's hotel. The party wasn't scheduled to begin for an hour and she wanted to be sure he understood how important this evening was to her.

"You can have the rest of the night off, Carlos."

"You sure?"

"Yes. Wade insisted on hiring a car and driver, since he is completely controlling."

"Don't know anyone else like that," Carlos said in a voice low enough she could pretend she hadn't heard him.

When she swept into the lobby of the hotel, even wearing a summer weight full-length coat that hid the glorious gown, she drew attention. She barely noticed as she headed for the elevator and then realized Wade hadn't even given her his room number.

It seemed particularly galling that the man she was engaged to wouldn't even share his hotel room number with her. She couldn't possibly ask the hotel front desk since she felt as though all of LA must be following the story of the curse and her sudden engagement.

She was about to call her fake fiancé when she saw a young woman who had the air of a Sarah Marsden in training carrying a florist's see-through box. One red boutonniere lay within it.

Gabby walked up to the woman. "Hello."

The young woman's eyes opened wide. "Hi, Evangeline. Wow."

Yes, definitely this one needed a bit of polish and sophistication yet. "You must work for Sarah?"

"I do. I'm Brie."

"Hi, Brie." She held out her hand. "I'm going to Mr. Davenport's room right now. I'll take that."

"Sure, of course. Um, Sarah asked me to make sure he'd reviewed his talking points."

"Don't worry. I'll take care of it. You get back to the ballroom and make sure everything is perfect. When Garry Greenstein gets there, I want him to be the happiest, most pampered man in LA." She took the floral box and confirmed the hotel room number was on the delivery label. "At least, until after his toast."

Brie laughed and, still looking a little starry-eyed, turned to leave.

When she got to Wade's hotel room door she took a moment to steady herself. They hadn't fought exactly, over him blurting out to *Cheerio!* that they couldn't come to the wedding, but they hadn't spoken since the interview, either. She needed him on good form tonight, she reminded herself, so she put on her best smile before knocking on the door.

He opened it and seemed taken aback to find her there. "Gabby! You're early."

"I know." Most likely he'd intended to meet her in the lobby. "May I come in?"

He hesitated for a second then said, "Of course."

He was dressed but for his bow tie and his jacket. He looked wonderful. If a bit distant, as though he didn't trust himself too close to her.

She followed him inside. Even though he'd booked a suite, with a galley kitchen, a real bedroom and a living area with a state-of-the-art workstation, she still thought he'd have been more comfortable at her house.

The TV was on with one of those twenty-four hour news and business stations playing softly. "You want a drink before we go?"

"No. I want to make sure you memorized your talking points."

His eyes gleamed briefly in amusement. "You want to run lines?"

"I want to make sure you don't embarrass me."

He turned back and stepped way up close, right in her personal space so they were all but touching. Even in her heels she had to tip her head to look him in the eye. "I will do my best not to embarrass you, but if you wanted a trained monkey to pretend he was going to marry you, you picked the wrong man." He picked up his tie, went to the mirror above a mahogany credenza, flipped up his shirt collar and slipped the black silk tie around his neck. Their gazes met in the mirror. "I am appearing in the media too, you know, and while I may not be a celebrity fashion designer, I do have clients and business associates who read papers, magazines, blogs and who watch TV." He shifted the tie so the ends were even. "Or they have wives or girlfriends or kids who do."

She hadn't thought of how this had affected his business. She'd been too busy thinking about her own business.

"If it's clear to everyone that I'm completely whipped, my clients are going to lose respect for me."

"I think whipped might be going a bit far."

"Do you?" he turned from the mirror and grabbed a computer printout. Shoved it at her. "This is my script of the things I'm allowed to say at my own engagement party."

Their gazes met and held. She could read his frustration.

And he'd been nice enough to cross the country to do her this huge favor. "I'm sorry," she said. "You can say whatever you want tonight."

When he would have turned back to the mirror, she stopped him and took on the job of tying his bow tie herself. How many times had she performed this task for him? She could smell the sandalwood from whatever soap he'd used, feel the warmth coming off his body. "Can I tell *Cheerio!* Magazine and anyone else who wants to come to our wedding that it's personal and they are not invited?"

She bit back a smile. She was not about to have a second argument about who was and was not invited to an event that wasn't going to take place. "You can."

"Thank you."

She finished his tie, then flipped the collar down over her handiwork. "There. You look very nice." And she lifted on tiptoe and gave him a quick kiss.

He gazed down at her. "Kissing a man in his hotel room is a good way to make us late for the party."

It was the expression in his eyes more than the words that made her heart rate speed up. "I thought this was strictly a favor from one old friend to another?"

He picked up his jacket and slipped it on. "I might be softening my position."

Men had begged to go out with her, they'd wooed her, flirted with her, one had stalked her to the point of a restraining order. They wrote poetry, film scripts they wanted her to star in, they sent flowers and jewelry and promised her the moon and stars. And Wade might be softening his position?

She raised her chin. "Lucky me."

His grin was swift and lethal and she realized she'd been played.

She reached for the florist's box. "I do understand how

awkward this is for you and I'm sorry. After the engagement party, things won't be so intense."

She slipped the red rose through his buttonhole and fixed it in place. "There." She didn't even glance at the speaking notes knowing she would have to trust Wade. "Shall we go?"

"Do I get a look at the goods first?" He eyed her coat.

"Oh." Ridiculous to feel slightly shy. "Of course." She unbuttoned the coat, feeling his eyes on her. The dress was cut low enough to be sexy, without being too revealing. It fell off her shoulders, clung where it touched. A woman who didn't work out as much as she did and watch her diet as rigorously could never have got away with it.

Wade gave a low whistle. "I'm a lucky man."

"That you are."

Before she could put the coat back on, he said, "Wait."

He disappeared into the bedroom and came back out holding a leather jewelry case. "Your engagement present."

Her startled gaze flew to his and she felt a blush forming. "Wade."

"We want to make this look real, don't we? And I can't have your fans and my associates thinking I don't know how to treat my future wife."

She flipped open the box with hands that weren't quite steady. "Oh, Wade, it's beautiful." The bracelet was diamond and ruby, tasteful and exquisite. He removed it from the case and she held out her hand for him to put it on her wrist. "How did you know?"

"I asked Sarah what color you'd be wearing."

"I love it. Thank you."

This was one of those foolish, awkward moments when a real couple would embrace and she had no idea how to respond. She said, "I have something for you, too, oddly enough. I'd intended it as a small thank-you gift, but we can consider it an engagement present." She went to her bag and retrieved her own jewelry box.

He glanced at her, then opened the box revealing gold cuff-links she'd had engraved with his initials.

"Perfect," he said, and held out his own wrists so she could replace the boring black cufflinks he was currently wearing in the French cuffed shirt with the gold ones.

When they left to meet his driver, he took her hand.

Within an hour of the party starting it was clear this was going to be a huge success. Everything was perfect, from the uniformed waiters carrying trays of champagne, exquisite hors d'oeuvres, the music, currently a string quartet, but later there would be a name band for dancing. She was conscious of looking her best and feeling well matched by the tall, handsome man beside her.

As Sarah had promised, everyone who was anyone was there, and in LA that made for a very glittering crowd. Celebri-ties from movies, music, modeling, sports, business and politics showed up to help her celebrate. The media who had been invited were the ones she considered the good guys. It wasn't that they wouldn't report on it if a star got involved in a DUI or ended up in rehab, but they didn't go out of their way to sling dirt, and were usually more interested in glitz and glamour.

And tonight was all glitz and glamour.

She hadn't expected to enjoy herself and was surprised at how much fun she had. Garry Greenstein's toast was both funny and warm hearted. He made fun of the curse, of the modeling industry, took a few gentle pokes at Manhattan busi-ness, and ended up by saying, "If this woman is cursed? I'll have what she's having." That pretty much brought the house down. He then raised his glass and said, "To Evangeline and Wade. God bless. Mazel tov."

There was resounding applause when he was finished and as

the noise died down, to her surprise, Wade took the mic. She searched for Sarah. Was this planned?

Then Wade began speaking. Maybe he wasn't one of the world's most famous and highly paid comedians, but she was surprised how confident and assured he was in front of this crowd. He thanked Garry for his kind words, and managed to get a good laugh himself when he described how fame had changed him. "A young woman at Starbucks asked me whether I was keeping my own name when we get married, or whether I'll be Mr. Evangeline." Most everyone in this room understood the strange encounters that being a celebrity or even associated with one caused. He spoke only briefly, thanking everyone for coming to the party. "Thank you for making this night so special for us."

Someone began clinking a glass and soon the sound grew. He laughed and pulled Gabby into his arms, planting her a good one. When he pulled away, everyone was clapping and laughing and she felt girlish and flushed. Wade said, "I didn't follow the script." His eyes were dancing with devilry.

"I noticed. You did good."

Then, even though the party had resumed and no one was particularly watching, he kissed her again, the kiss of a man with a lot more on his mind than kissing.

She wrapped her arms around him and clung. She'd missed this so much, missed him.

She kept mingling, making an extra effort to talk to all the reporters who hadn't already left to file stories and upload photographs. This party was mainly for them, after all.

This room contained some of the best looking men in the world. They were A-list actors, models, athletes, but not one of them made her pulse race the way a certain stubborn man from Manhattan did.

The party was winding down, when Wade appeared at her elbow. He guided her away from the drunk TV actor currently trying to seduce her. At least, that's what she thought he was attempting, he was so wasted it was difficult to be certain.

He very neatly substituted Sarah's assistant Brie, introducing her to the drunk actor and easing Gabby away.

"Oh, poor Brie."

"She'll be fine. And at least she's getting paid for this gig."

"True."

"You ready to get out of here?"

Oh, she was, especially if it meant she could finally be alone with Wade. She'd felt him seducing her all night with little touches, his gaze scorching her skin every time she caught him looking at her. "I feel like we should wait until more people have left."

He shook his head. "I checked with Sarah Marsden. She gave us the green light to slip away."

She'd always been one to arrive fashionably late and leave a party before it grew boring. To have permission to slip away from her very own party seemed fitting.

"Great. I'll get my coat."

Soon they were in the back of his car. "Would you care to come back to my place?" He didn't offer an excuse, like a drink or something, but then it was very clear to both of them what he had in mind.

"I would like that very much," she murmured. And, with a very satisfied expression on his face, he gave the order to the driver.

He took her hand in his. The bracelet winked and sparkled. "I had so many compliments on the bracelet. Thank you."

He lifted her hand, turned it over and pressed his lips to her wrist. "You're welcome."

He didn't lunge at her in the back of the car, even though she could feel the pent up wanting, instead, he tortured her senses. The kiss on the sensitive skin on the inside of her wrist, a finger tracing the line of her hip.

By the time they got to his hotel she was so hot she was melting.

They headed straight to his room and when he had the door shut behind them, he swiftly unbuttoned her coat, letting it slip to the floor. "You looked like a fire goddess tonight in your red dress," he said, before kissing her deeply.

She made an incoherent sound and kissed him back.

"We never did practice my talking points," he said, as he kissed his way to spot where her breasts met above the fabric of her dress and put his mouth there.

She could hardly manage a sensible thought. "Talking points?"

"Mmm." He took her hand, scooped up the printout and led her into the bedroom.

What on earth?

"Talking point one," he turned her and, instead of unzipping the dress, kissed that point at the top of her spine that made her shiver. "Evangeline is an amazing woman. I'm proud of her success." He slid the zipper slowly, slowly south.

This dress had been made for her and a bra would have ruined the line. She could almost feel his lust spike when he realized she was braless.

"Talking point two," He traced the line of her spine with one finger. "We'll keep houses in both LA and New York."

He slipped the dress down her arms and let it slide. "Talking point three," and then as it slid all the way his tone thickened. "You're not wearing any underwear."

She chuckled, thrilled at how his lust was choking him. "That's quite a sound bite."

He turned her slowly. She felt nervous and fluttery. "I'm not twenty anymore," she warned. As hard as she worked out and as rigorously as she monitored her diet, twenty years had taken their toll. Her skin tone wasn't as firm, her breasts were fuller and softer. She had ripened.

He was still fully dressed and she was naked but for a pair of silver heels. "You are more beautiful than ever." And then he drew her to him and kissed her.

As he'd undressed her, she returned the favor, but the teasing was over. Need and long pent up desire pulled at them. He scrambled out of his formal wear, and she helped, relieving him of his cufflinks.

He also looked better than he had in his twenties. He'd filled out, carried himself with added assurance.

When he tipped her back on the bed, so familiar and yet so new, she wondered how she had ever gone so long without him.

Then he put his mouth to her breast and she was lost to all thought for a very long time.

CHAPTER 11

*G*abby turned up at work on Monday heavy eyed and very, very satisfied. She and Wade had barely left his bed until this morning when she'd scampered home to change her clothes before heading into Evangeline.

She made the rounds of her design house, complimenting the seamstresses on their attention to detail, offering a helpful suggestion to the pattern maker who took her designs and turned them into workable cutting patterns. She became rapturous over a bolt of ivory satin that had arrived that morning from Milan.

If she was conscious of the astonished glances of her staff—no, her team—she pretended to be oblivious. She wondered if Wade and Sarah Marsden were correct and she'd have happier and more productive employees if she truly believed they were a team. It was something to think about.

Her day seemed to fly by with none of the usual snags and complications. When Marlene and Leandra arrived at two in the afternoon, Gabby had almost forgotten they were scheduled for the smudge session.

She was wearing one of her favorite dresses, a soft gray silk that felt wonderful against her skin and would be ridiculously easy to remove. She and Wade had made no plans for after work, but she definitely had some ideas.

Marlene strode in looking as though she were wearing John Travolta's white suit from Saturday Night Fever. With her flame red hair cascading down, the effect was startling.

Leandra was much smaller but equally colorful. She looked to be in her sixties and wore a loose paisley blouse, a flowing black cotton skirt and sandals. On her head Leandra wore a blue and red silk scarf wrapped around her hair turban style. She wore no makeup. She did not need it with those large, penetrating almost-black eyes.

The four young brides, or wives, she supposed apart from the redheaded Megan O'Reilly, filed in together. She got the feeling they had met first, maybe even shared a ride. Kate and Ashley she knew, so she introduced herself to Tasmine Ford, who shook her hand heartily as though they'd just finished engaging in some sort of sport together. And, finally, Megan, who was much more tentative in her greeting, but stared at her with appeal in her dark brown eyes.

The thought flicked through her mind that the Tarot card reading had mentioned a light-haired woman. And Megan's red hair had a lot of gold in it.

She was glad to see there was no awkwardness between Marlene and Kate Winton-Jones. In fact, for all the complicated relationships in this room, everyone seemed at ease with everyone else. Marlene introduced herself to Tasmine and Meg, and Leandra watched them all.

She gazed around the space and her gaze caught on the wedding gown hanging in the corner. "Is that the dress? The cursed dress?"

They all turned to stare at the dress, so exquisite, so unloved. "It is."

"Good. Now, ladies, gather round." The women gathered

around her in a loose circle. Ashley said to her, "I really like your turban. Is that part of your costume?"

Leandra laughed. "Oh, bless you. No. I can't stand the smell of smoke in my hair. I wrap the silk around my head so I don't come home smelling like I've spent the night out back of a bar huddled in the smoker's corner."

She glanced at all of them and had them repeat their names to her, taking a moment to stare into each woman's eyes just until the gaze became uncomfortable and then she'd move on. When she had given them each the piercing stare routine, she nodded briskly. She opened her bag and withdrew what looked like a bundle of straw that was about six inches long and tied together so it made a dense bundle about an inch thick. Kind of like a very ragged cigar made of weeds. "What we're going to need is an open window." She strode to the long French doors that opened onto the balcony, and pushed them open wide. Light streamed in, gleaming on the rich, hardwood floors and Gabby was surprised to see the sun. Something about this woman and this ceremony called for moonlight.

Leandra waved the unlit bundle so they could all see it. "This is a smudge stick. Now I don't want you to worry that it's been polluted with any kind of bad thoughts. I have a very few good provider who assures me this sage is pure. But, all of us carry energy in with us and so, before I start, with your permission, I will smudge each of us." The women all looked around at each other and nodded or shrugged.

"Good." Leandra dug around in her bag. Gabby could hear clanking sounds and crystals banging on crystals. She wondered what was in there. Leandra gave a frustrated *tsk*. "I always forget something. I forgot my lighter. Does anyone have a lighter? Or some matches?"

No one spoke for a moment. Kate Winton-Jones said, "Sorry, I don't smoke."

"Me either," Ashley said.

Tasmine shrugged healthy cheerleader shoulders and shook her head. It only needed one glance at that clear healthy skin to know that woman never smoked a cigarette in her life.

"Sorry," Megan O'Reilly said. Since Megan was here under false pretenses in the first place, Gabby felt that the least she could have done was to be a smoker.

Well, she wasn't going to waste the afternoon after all the trouble she had gone to get all these people gathered in one place, not for the lack of a damn match.

She strode over to her Chippendale desk and dragged open the lowest drawer. She pulled out a package of matches that advertised the Waldorf-Astoria. She pushed the drawer shut with her knee and walked back over presenting the matches on her open palm.

"Oh, aren't you a sweetie. I thought for a moment someone was going have to run down to the corner store for a penny book of matches."

She struck the wooden match against the flinty thing with gusto and the red tip sprang into flame. She held the lit match against the sage bundle, turning it to make sure every bit of it lit and she held it up for a moment until it was good and flaming and then she blew out the flame. What was left was a lazily smoking hunk of weed. It smelled a bit sweet and mildly like mold. "The native peoples use this particular sage because the smell is reminiscent of the earth," Leandra said.

Or beach parties.

"Now, I'll start the spiritual cleansing with myself." As she spoke she began waving the smoking sage stick down her arms, over her body, up and down her legs and around her turban-clad head.

"Marlene? You okay to go next?"

"Sure." Marlene gathered her long, red hair in one hand. "Wish I'd thought to bring a silk scarf, though." Then she stood by while Leandra smudged her.

Then she moved toward Kate Winton-Jones and began the same procedure. She got to Tasmine Ford when suddenly the door opened and in walked Wade, carrying a bouquet of flowers and saying, "I snuck past Salvador, I thought we'd—"

He stopped dead on the threshold and gaped at the seven women gathered in a smoky circle. She felt color climb into her cheeks and jumped as though she'd been caught doing something reprehensible. "Wade! I wasn't expecting you."

He recovered in an instant and gazed lazily at the proceedings as though he witnessed smudge ceremonies every day. "Ladies," he said nodding slightly. "Sorry to interrupt. Evangeline, call me later." He was about to leave when Leandra stopped him. "No. No. If you're here, it's because you're meant to be. Please come in and shut the door behind you."

He glanced up in mild horror. As his gaze connected with Gabby's, she stifled the urge to giggle. "It's a smudge ceremony, darling. Leandra is trying to rid my space of bad energy."

"I should've guessed."

Leandra motioned him to stand beside Megan O'Reilly. Eyeing the smoking sage, he removed his jacket and placed it on a far chair. He wore a crisp white dress shirt. She could see from the glint of gold that he was wearing the cufflinks she'd given him. His trousers were gray and his black loafers shiny. She introduced him. "Everyone, this is my fiancé, Wade Davenport. Wade, in order from the left are Kate Winton-Jones, Ashley Carnarvon, Tasmine Ford and Megan O'Reilly. I'm not sure who's changed their names when they got married, but we'll use first names."

He nodded at all of them. "Pleased to meet you."

"And this is Marlene in the white suit and Leandra is leading the smudge ceremony."

Leandra had finished with Megan by this time and so she turned to Wade. "I'm just going to smudge you, Wade. Is that all right?"

"I thought you'd never ask." He could flirt with anybody and get away with it. Leandra giggled. "I like a man who's a good sport." As she was speaking she was running the smoking stick around his body and up and down his legs. She had to reach up on her tiptoes to get near the top of his head. "My aren't you a tall drink of water on a hot day."

Finally, she carried the smoking stick to Gabby. "Evangeline, honey, it's your turn."

She wished that Leandra had smudged her first so that she wouldn't have to stand here like a fish in a smokehouse while Wade watched her with that teasing expression in his eyes. Besides, all that sweet acrid smoke reminded her how desperately she wanted to grab that pack of Players in the back of her drawer and smoke every one of them.

Once she'd well and truly smoked Gabby, Leandra walked towards the dress in the corner.

"Do you mind if I smudge the dress?"

"Do you have to?" Now, on top of everything else, she'd have to get the dress dry-cleaned.

"If the dress was cursed, then yes, I really need to smudge it."

"Fine." She sighed. This was such a terrible idea; she never should have listened to Marlene.

After Leandra had circled the dress waving her weedy cigar and puffs of smoke wafted around it as though the gown were being burned at the stake she nodded and returned. "Now ladies and gentleman I'd like you to come and stand in a circle near the dress. I will walk around the room and I'll recite a little incantation that will invite any darkness, any anger or pain to leave the space and replace it only with harmony and peace. I want you all to think peaceful, joyful thoughts as you listen to my words." Her voice took on a hypnotic quality, or maybe she was getting high from the smoke. "Visualize any darkness, any anger, floating out those windows and being replaced by calm and peace and joy."

It was difficult to think peaceful thoughts when Wade was so close and all she could do was relive her amazing weekend, but she tried.

The woman walked slowly to the center of the room. She raised the stick towards the ceiling and chanted, "Spirits of the North, I call on all you to release any darkness or pain from this space and replace it with peace and joy," then she moved the stick in the opposite direction and recited, "Spirits of the South, I call on all you to release any darkness or pain from this space and replace it with peace and joy," she repeated the words, pointing her stick twice more and then she moved to a corner and began her incantation again. Wade interrupted, "Leandra, I hope you don't mind me saying, but you need a compass. That's not north, it's east."

Leandra giggled one more time. "Oh dear. I've never had much sense of direction. Did I get any of the directions right?"

He shook his head.

"Well, I don't want the poor spirits to get all confused and spin around in circles bumping into each other." She said to Wade, "Maybe you can chant with me." She walked over and linked her arm with his and dragged him with her. Her silk turban had tilted so it was hanging over one eyebrow and she looked more like a pirate with a smoking problem than any kind of spiritual healer.

"Spirits of the North?" She gazed at Wade inquiringly and he pointed her to north. Then he pointed to south and so they continued. Wade was like a spiritual seeing-eye dog giving her a nudge so she knew where she was going and Leandra and her smudge stick obligingly followed his directions for north and south and east and west. She glanced over and saw that Ashley and Tasmine were getting red in the face from stifling giggles and she felt a wild urge to guffaw like she used to in the old days. The smoke hung lazily and there was a slight haze in the atmosphere when Leandra and Wade returned to the circle.

"Now, I'm going to walk around this whole circle and to the dress particularly and Evangeline and I want you all to work with me. Together we'll visualize any kind of bad energy floating out that window."

They all nodded solemnly. Though Ashley's eyes were filled with tears of unexpressed merriment she managed a nod.

Leandra didn't notice the suppressed hilarity or chose to ignore it. Once more she walked around the circle saying her piece and, even though Gabby felt that this was the most ridiculous spectacle she'd ever taken part in, she repeated the words in her head.

And then the most remarkable thing happened. She was idly watching Leandra follow Wade's directions as she did her north, south, east and west business, when suddenly the lazy smoldering resolved itself into a solid stream of smoke and while they all watched, open mouthed, it turned a lazy corkscrew and disappeared out the open window. For a stunned moment no one said a thing, including Leandra.

"Well I'll be damned," Wade said at last.

Ashley blinked. "That was the absolute coolest thing I have ever seen."

No one else said a word. Marlene walked up to Leandra and gave her a big hug. "That was awesome."

Leandra took in a big breath and let it out again and then, very carefully, she put out her smoldering smudge stick and presented it to Gabby. "You can keep this, dear. Anytime you feel a need to cleanse the space, you can follow what I did."

She accepted the gift gingerly, then placed it on a crystal dish where she kept spare pins.

Marlene walked to the center of the room and turned around. She nodded. "I can feel it, can't you? The anger and bad feeling is gone and all I sense is peace and harmony."

Gabby was desperate to believe it was true and if some crazy woman in a silk scarf and dangling crystal earrings was literally blowing smoke, she didn't care. She wanted to believe she was free of the bad luck and bad press that had dogged her. "Is it gone? Does this mean the curse is gone?"

Leandra shrugged. "Whatever bad energy was in this room is gone. Curses aren't really my area."

She began packing up her bag and Marlene made a gesture rubbing her thumb against fingers reminding Gabby that curses might not be Leandra's thing but money certainly was. She reached into her desk drawer and pulled out the check that she'd already had prepared. She passed it to Leandra. "Thank you very much."

The woman tucked the check into her bag and then took Gabby by the shoulders and looked deep into her eyes again for that one moment beyond comfort. Then she pulled her in for a smoke scented hug. "You're going to be okay. I can see it."

For a second she hugged the woman back. "I hope so."

CHAPTER 12

*M*arlene and Leandra left first. The four brides seemed as though they didn't quite know what to do with themselves. Gabby supposed that if she were a better host she would offer them a cup of tea or a glass of wine or something but she wanted them all to go away. Wade didn't barge into her office carrying flowers for no reason.

Besides, she felt a little too stunned by the way that smoke had turned and headed out the window. She needed some time to process that.

Tasmine, Ashley and Kate huddled together for a moment and then Ashley said, "I don't know about you guys, but I could sure use a drink. We're going down the road to Señor Hooch for margaritas. Who wants to come?"

She couldn't stand the thought of sitting, making jokes over salt-rimmed glasses with these women. However, they'd gone to a great deal of trouble to be here for her. Wade did not say anything. He looked at her, and she felt as though he were testing her somehow. She hated it when he looked at her like that. Almost always, whatever it was he expected, she screwed it up. Well, the least she could do was to buy these girls a drink.

She dug her wallet out of her bag and pulled out a couple of fifties. Ever since she'd been young she had understood the value of always having a substantial amount of cash in her possession. She'd never lost the habit. She walked to Kate who, as the first of the brides, was appointed leader. She said, "I'm sorry, girls, I've got too much work to do today. But please, let me buy you a drink." She handed the money to Kate who looked at the bills as though she had never seen currency before and then up at Gabby with a slightly puzzled expression on her face. "That's okay. We don't need your money."

She felt that she had made some sort of social blunder, something she tried very hard not to do. She crumpled the bills in her hand. "Well, I am sorry I can't join you. Perhaps next time."

"Yeah," Ashley said. "Next time we smudge a dark spirit out of here we'll get another drink."

Tasmine laughed and looked inquiringly at Megan. The redhead glanced after the three longingly and said, "Is it okay if I join you there? I want to talk to Evangeline."

"Sure, see you later."

OH NO. She did not want to have this conversation. There was a reason she had wished not to include Megan O'Reilly in this curse-busting session. But, the girl had come over here specially. She owed her a meeting. She dragged up a smile. "Wade, could you give us a minute?"

"Sure," he said.

Megan shook her head and the sun caught that gorgeous red hair sparking bronze and copper. "Oh no, that's okay. He can stay. It won't take that long."

She shrugged. Put the professional smile back on her face.

She refused even to glance at the dress hanging there slightly smoky but curse free. "What can I do for you?"

Megan took a deep breath and pushed her hair behind her ears in what was clearly a nervous gesture. "I'm sure you know why I'm here. I've been trying to get hold of you." Even as Gabby refused to so much as glance at the dress hanging in the corner, Megan seemed unable to stop staring at the gown. "I wonder if you'd consider, if there's anything I could do, to encourage you to let me wear that dress for my wedding."

The girl was absolutely beautiful in a quirky, non-traditional kind of way. Exactly the kind of face and body that would normally make her fingers itch to design for. How to handle this delicate situation. "Of course I would love for you to wear it except that I've already announced to all the world that I will be wearing that dress myself when I get married."

Those lovely shoulders slumped ever so slightly. "I know. You did say that. But, so often the things that celebrities say in the press and what they really do are different. It was worth a shot."

A tug of compassion pulled out her. "I can't let you wear this dress." The very idea of her planning a wedding and not turning up for the ceremony was too much to even contemplate. Evangeline's business and her reputation hung by a thread as it was. If one more bride spurned that dress, it would all be over. However, she could be generous. She said, "But I'll do something even better. I will design you your own dress. I think we could do something absolutely stunning."

She'd expected the girl to beam with happiness, weep with joy, jump up and down with excitement; instead her shoulders slumped a little more. "I don't want another dress. I want this dress." She fumbled in her purse and pulled out a satin-covered photo album. She passed it to Gabby. "Please, just look at these."

She opened the album and saw that it was filled with photographs of Megan wearing the dress. In every pose, whether candid or studied, the dress and Megan seemed to reflect each other's glory.

There was one she particularly liked of Megan and the young man who looked enough like Joanne West that she knew this must be her son. He was lifting Megan in the air and the two of them looked so happy to be in each other's arms that her heart did tug a little.

The dress she had designed for Kate Winton-Jones looked as though it had actually been made for Megan O'Reilly. It was as though the gown had found its true owner. But she couldn't risk her business, everything she'd built and worked for, not for one starry-eyed girl wearing a dress that should never have been hers. Even so, she flipped through the rest of the photos in the album. Here was this lovely girl reclining on a red velvet settee and the equally photogenic young man slipping a ring onto her finger. Megan came up beside her and said, "That's Dylan. That's the man I'm going to marry." Even her voice trembled with sincerity. As if she couldn't tell from the photographs that these two were in love.

Wade did not say a word. He was sitting at her desk and she thought he might be checking email on his phone, but she felt his presence. She hesitated for just a moment and then said, with complete honesty, "I'm sorry. If it had only been one bride who didn't wear this dress down the aisle, I might take the chance, but it's been three brides. If you took the dress and didn't get married, I could never recover." She had to make this girl understand that her generosity only went so far. "Please, let me design you another gown. On the house."

"I wish I could describe to you how it felt when I wore that dress. How everything seemed right."

"My dear girl, that dress was cursed. No one ever gets married in it. It's the last dress you should want."

She shook her head. "I don't think so. I think—and I know this sounds crazy—but I think maybe that dress has magic. But not black magic. Do you think Kate Winton-Jones would have been happy if she'd married Edward Carnarvon? I've talked to all of these brides. We got to know each other because we're all involved with that dress. Do you think Ashley Carnarvon would have been married happily to Eric van Hoffendam?" She shook her head. "She and Ben Saegar are like soul mates and Tasmine is perfect for Eric. I was at their wedding. You have never seen such intense love."

"I am very happy they all found happiness, I really am. But I have paid a heavy price for these women who couldn't make up their minds. I'm sorry, I can't be made a fool of again."

Megan heaved a sigh, and gazed at the gown as though it were her lover heading off to war and she had no idea if she'd ever see it again. "Well, at least I tried."

She felt that she had failed somehow. Wade's dispassionate gaze on her made her somehow feel that she was standing in front of the angel Gabriel, or whoever stood at the pearly gates. He was standing there holding up a list and it wasn't looking good for her. She said, "The offer stands. I am willing to design you a stunning gown. Do you know how many women around the world would kill for a chance like this?"

Megan smiled sadly. "I appreciate it, I really do. But it wouldn't be the same."

"We could start fitting today. I could have your gown finished in four weeks."

Why was she begging for this girl's charity business? Megan shook her head once more. "No, thank you."

She felt an unfamiliar sense of desperation. She wanted to close this deal. "Two weeks. I can put a rush on it and have it done in two weeks. You're surely not getting married in the next fortnight?"

But Megan was already walking to the door. As she was leaving she took a final glance at the dress. "I just wanted the magic."

CHAPTER 13

$\mathcal{A}$s the door closed she felt the echo of finality. She glanced up at Wade. "Well, I don't know what more I could have done."

He looked at her with cool gray eyes. "You could have let her wear that dress. You know damn well you're never going to wear it." He'd placed the bouquet of flowers on the desktop. She wanted to thank him but she needed to get things straight first.

"It's imperative that the world believes I will be wearing it." She walked over to him, beseeching him to understand. "You know better than anyone how hard it's been for me. How hard I worked to become not only a top model but a top designer. What were the chances that little Gabby Brock would end up with all of this?" She raised her arm and extended it like an interior designer showing off a newly decorated room. "The chances were nonexistent. I had no business to make a success of myself."

He stood and put his hands on her shoulders. "And yet you did. And I've been proud of you. For all the crazy roller coaster ride you've put me through, I have always been proud of what you've done."

She finished the sentence for him, "But not today?"

"Not today. You had a chance to give that girl magic. Magic's a very special thing. You can't hold it in your hand, you can't put it in a jar or lock it in a safe. It's as fleeting as a shooting star."

"Well, if she's so in love with the man from the vintage store she'll have plenty of magic. It's not the wedding dress that makes a marriage, you know."

"Oh, I know."

She looked up to Wade. The energy in the room had shifted somewhat. She felt almost as though a cold breeze floated in from the window, which was crazy since it was seventy degrees outside and sunny. But something had shifted. She put her arms around Wade's neck and rubbed up against him like a cat.

"Let's not argue. I'm sure you didn't come here to get smoked like a side of bacon. I'm sure we can think of something more interesting to talk about."

He gazed down at her for a moment and she felt her heart speed up. He didn't look like he wanted to take her to bed, he looked as though he had something much more serious in mind. He pushed her gently away. "I came here to tell you something."

She took a step back instinctively as she prepared for bad news. "I'm listening."

He pushed his hands in his pockets but even through the fabric she could see that they were clenched. "I have to get back to New York. I got a call this morning. There's an emergency they need me for in person." He blew out a breath. "To be honest with you I never intended to stay this long in the first place."

She nodded. She had always known this would happen. He didn't need to look so serious. "That's fine. When do you leave?"

"Tonight."

Her eyebrows rose. "So soon?"

"We'll have an emergency meeting tomorrow, first thing."

In the old days he'd have told her exactly what was happening. Now he didn't.

She nodded. She understood business. "When will you be back?"

He took a step towards the window. She could see his outline against the light, the strong shoulders, the torso she loved to wrap her arms around, his long legs. She even liked the way he held his head. "I won't be coming back." He said the words to the window and she felt them floating out the way the smoke from the smudge stick had.

"What do you mean, you won't be coming back? What about our weekend? Surely we aren't finished with each other."

He shook his head, still looking away from her and then finally he turned. She was shocked at the blazing expression in his eyes. He said, "I love you, Gabby. I have loved you from the beginning, when you were a scrappy young model, all long legs and big eyes, trying to find your place in the world. I've admired you and I've supported you wherever I could. But the woman I love is Gabby Brock. I can appreciate that Evangeline is a marketing creation and she's brilliant, but she was never meant to take over."

She attempted to laugh but it came out sounding like a strange rusty sound. "You make me seem like some sort of horror film."

"Sometimes that's how this feels. This amazing, vital, honest woman has turned into this slick marketing-driven machine."

Her eyes clouded with tears, which infuriated her. "I'm not a machine. I'm a woman doing my best and I'm a company owner. If this company goes down it's not only me, but the people who work with me. Don't I have an obligation to care about them?"

He raised one eyebrow. "All these people who work *with* you? Suddenly it's *with*?"

"Wade. Please. Are you saying the engagement's off?" Her heart felt strangely as though it were tearing. Slowly and painfully.

He shook his head. "What engagement? This was a publicity stunt. You asked me for a favor and I did it. You never had any intention of marrying me. But you know what's sad? We had that magic, exactly the magic Megan O'Reilly was talking about. We had it twenty years ago and we got it back this weekend."

"This weekend was amazing."

"But when you took away that girl's magic, I saw that you are the one cursing yourself. I'm right here and I'm telling you I love you. Are you ready to deal with a real man, who actually loves you and wants to make a life with you?"

The seconds ticked by. He loved her. Somehow, she'd always known that, but never expected him to push her like this, to offer an ultimatum. She felt lost, confused. How could he say he loved her and sound so angry? "What am I going to do without you?" She was surprised at her own words. When had she come to need him? To depend on him? She had never been needy. Never.

He came forward until they were almost touching. It was as though he'd read her thoughts. "You've never needed anyone." He leaned down and kissed her with all the sweetness and pain of goodbye. "Take care of yourself, Gabby."

And while she stood there, stunned, he strode over, scooped his jacket off the chair and walked out.

She glanced up at the dress as though it were a friend and said, "Well, it's a good thing we got all that bad energy cleared out of here."

A breeze wafted in and set the dress to quivering. She felt as though it were shaking its head at her. She shook a finger right back. "Don't you dare disapprove of me. I made you and I can take a pair of scissors to you."

That's what she should do. She should get a pair of scissors and cut this thing into ribbons. But she knew she wouldn't. Maybe they were only satin and lace, but to her each one of her gowns represented a dream.

The truth hit her so hard she sat down with a bang. Every dress fulfilled a dream. The trouble with this dress was that it was always in the wrong dream. What had she done? Kate Winton-Jones was never meant to marry Ted Carnarvon. Ashley Carnarvon was never meant to marry Eric Van Hoffendam because he was meant to marry Tasmine Ford. Megan O'Reilly was probably meant to marry Dylan West.

As she sat there, another fact struck her with blinding clarity. It was that Gabby Brock was meant to marry Wade Davenport. Her hands began to tremble as she took the dress down from where it hung in the romance corner of her newly Feng Shui'd studio. She carried it to the corner where she did her fittings and called two seamstresses to come up.

When they arrived she felt breathless and agitated. In the mirror she could see her face was flushed. She said, "Hurry, I need you to help me into this stress. I mean dress."

They glanced at each other and she could see that they were surprised by the request but she didn't have time to explain. She was seized by a sense of urgency. She began tossing off her own clothes. Normally she was so careful. She'd known what it was like when a ten dollar vintage store purchase was a great deal of money. She had never lost her need to take care of her clothes. But not today. She tossed off her gray dress, sending it sailing through the air in the direction of a chair.

While she was undressing, Annabelle, who had recently graduated from the New York School of Fashion Design, and Jennifer, who had apprenticed to a designer in London, sprang to attention. Annabelle held the dress while Jennifer unbuttoned the tiny little buttons down the back. Now Gabby was down to a bra, lacy panties and a pair of cream heels. They helped her step into the dress, pulled it up and swiftly redid the buttons. She turned to stare at the reflection of herself in the mirror. She had always loved this dress, it was one of her favorite creations. What she should do was to swallow her pride, beg Wade to return and marry him. As she'd announced she would. And she would wear this dress.

And then she saw her reflection in the mirror. The gown simply didn't fit. Not only was it too big in the body, it wasn't long enough. Plus, she was very long-waisted and this dress had been designed for a woman with a shorter spine.

It was for a shorter woman altogether. On her six-foot frame, the dress was cocktail length. For a woman who had been an acknowledged beauty all her life, this was the first time she'd ever felt like the ugly stepsister.

She was inserting herself into a dress that didn't fit as pigheadedly as Cinderella's stepsisters had tried to stuff their much bigger feet into her glass slipper.

She had a moment when she realized what Wade had been trying to tell her. She was killing herself to save Evangeline, who was more fantasy than reality. And underneath, the real Gabby was perfectly good in her own right. That's what someone should have told those ugly stepsisters. Out there somewhere was a shoe that would fit them, too.

But it wasn't this one.

Evangeline and Gabby were not the same person. All the times she had tried to squish Gabby into nonexistence to become this fantasy she created, all she'd done was make herself unhappy. And, to her horror, she realized, as she stood there staring at herself with her mouth open, that she may have chased away the one man in the whole world who had always seen her exactly as she was. And he loved her.

He loved Gabby Brock. Because he knew her. He really knew her and he hadn't run screaming. He liked her horse laugh and her ambition and her energy. And she'd let him go. "Oh dear, oh dear," she said to the reflection.

Annabel and Jennifer both hastened to reassure her. Annabelle's nimble fingers pinched the fabric of the bodice. "We can take in the seams and get it to fit right."

Jennifer nodded. "Add a band of fabric to the bottom, perhaps. We could sew a line of pearls to hide the seam. We can make this work." They were not frightened of her, they seemed genuinely anxious to please her and make her happy.

She hugged each of them in turn, quickly and awkwardly, because it was very unusual for her to do this. And each of them stepped back looking slightly confused and wary. She shook her head with determination. "No. Get me out of this dress now. I'm not wearing it, and I'm in a hurry."

They scrambled to comply and within minutes she was back in her own clothes. She grabbed her purse. "Thank you, girls. I appreciate you helping me today."

And then she ran out the door. As her heels clicked on the pavement, she tried to remember the name of the tequila place. She hadn't really paid attention because she'd had no intention of going. They'd said it was a block away, but in which direction? She passed a high-end florist she sometimes patronized, a bakery that might be new, and, tucked away as though embarrassed to be in such an upscale neighborhood, a blue and yellow sign with a very bad sombrero and a cactus a five-year-old might have painted. Señor Hooch. Really? There was a place near Evangeline Design called Señor Hooch?

And four lovely young women had chosen to spend their afternoon in such a place? She shrugged her shoulders and entered the dimly lit restaurant bar. There was a shaded patio out back and she could see through the restaurant to where four girls were sitting out there. An African-American man wearing a sombrero came up and said, "Hola. Can I get you a table?"

She shook her head. "I'm meeting some friends. I can see them sitting out there on the patio."

She strode through the restaurant, relieved they were still here, but with a feeling of urgency still upon her. She burst through the doors and onto the patio. Ashley saw her first and stopped in mid sentence, her mouth falling open as she gaped in shock.

Gabby pulled up a confident smile. "I hope the invitation is still open? I suddenly realized I am dying for a margarita. I haven't been able to stop thinking about it since you girls left."

Now the four of them all turned to stare at her. Kate recovered first. "Yes, of course. We're so glad you could join us." From the slightly stiff faces and awkward silence she felt positive they'd been discussing her. Not that she could really blame them. She had brought them all together and it had been rather a colorful afternoon. They shuffled their seats to make room for a fifth person, but there were only four chairs with the table. She strode over to a nearby table where two women sat a table for four. "Excuse me, do you mind if I take this chair?"

"No," and then one of the women gaped at her. "Oh, my, aren't you . . . ?"

She smiled suddenly at them. "I used to be." And she took the chair. By this time someone had managed to signal the waiter and almost as soon as she'd settled herself, a large frosty margarita was placed in front of her. She could see that the girls were nearly finished their drinks. She said, "And another round for everybody."

She sipped her margarita, enjoying the salty sweet tang. There was awkward silence for a moment apart from the tinny jangle of a mariachi band from the outdoor speakers. Then, Ashley Carnarvon said, "That was amazing what Leandra did."

She nodded, putting her glass down and licking salt off her lip. "It was amazing. But I had an epiphany after you all left. No, worse, I took a look at myself in the mirror and I didn't like what I saw."

The four women glanced among themselves and she felt their discomfort. She laughed. To her surprise, it wasn't her usual well-modulated Evangeline giggle but a full belly Gabby laugh. "Oh, don't worry. I'm not about to have some emotional meltdown at a place called Señor Hooch. I had a moment and I felt I wanted to be here with all of you."

"Isn't your fiancé waiting for you?" Tasmine asked.

The pain hit her, swift and sharp. "No, he left. He's gone back to New York."

"On business?"

For a moment she was tempted to unburden herself to these four women she barely knew. But years of living in the public eye prevented the impulse before it bloomed. She said, "Of course, he'll be back soon."

She took another sip of her margarita and then said the words she had come here to say. She looked at Megan who had been following the conversation with interest but had yet to say a word. "Megan, I've been thinking about what you said. About magic and weddings. Every wedding gown I design is part of a fairy tale. I've always felt that each gown was perfect for its bride." The three women who had not worn the gown all dropped their gazes to their drinks. She couldn't help but smile. "I think this gown has a little extra magic. It wasn't right for any of you three. And, frankly, I just tried it on and it's not right for me either. You were right, Megan. That dress is yours."

Even though her heart was heavy with grief knowing that Wade had gone and wasn't coming back, she couldn't help but be a tiny bit happy when Megan jumped up out of her seat with a squeal of joy, ran around the table and threw her arms around Gabby in an impulsive hug. "Oh my gosh, thank you so much. You don't know how much this means to me. I mean, of course I was going to marry Dylan anyway and having the right dress isn't going to make or break a marriage, I understand that, but, there was just something about that dress and the way it brought me and Dylan together that, well, I'm babbling, but it just seemed like it was meant to be."

"I know." Gabby reached into her bag and pulled out the wedding album with the photographs of Megan in the gown with her fiancé. She passed the album over. "You forgot this in my studio."

Megan received the album as though it were something precious that would break her heart to lose. "Thank you so much. I don't know how I came to forget it."

"You were a bit upset. It's easy to lose things when you let your emotions get in the way." And who knew better than she? How had she let the most important thing in her life slip through her fingers by being so closed-minded, so focused on her business that she hadn't paid attention to her heart?

Who cared if Evangeline never designed another gown? Who cared if some nasty little paparazzi made her life hell? In the big picture? She had everything she wanted without seeing it, and if she didn't do something, and fast, she was going to lose it all.

Maybe she couldn't fix what she'd broken, but at least she could help make one young bride very happy.

In fact, all the women looked ridiculously happy as though *they* were the ones getting a perfect wedding dress. Of course, all of them had had that wedding dress; they just hadn't worn it.

Megan glanced around the table, her brown eyes gleaming and her cheeks prettily flushed. "You all have to come to my wedding. In fact, would it be too strange for me to ask you all to be bridesmaids?" And then she clamped her lips shut as though she'd said the wrong thing.

They all glanced at each other around the table. And then Ashley started to laugh. "Why not? I think that's a great idea. Even though none of us knew each other before, I feel like the dress brought us together and maybe we were all meant to be friends." Because she was feeling in an expansive mood and everyone looked so happy, Gabby said, "I'll design the bridesmaid dresses if you like. Something that would look stunning on each of you and coordinate with Megan's gown."

Meg looked as though her cup was full to overflowing with

bliss. "I'm not even waiting for the others to answer. I say YES! I know you're getting married yourself, and you're a celebrity and everything, but would you consider maybe being in the wedding party?"

She was about to refuse, making some charming excuse, when she realized that in the whole course of her life no one had ever asked her to be a bridesmaid. That beautiful gown had been on such a journey and all of them had been part of it, had been changed by it. She glanced up, "Yes. I would love to be a bridesmaid."

Megan was so excited she was jumping up and down on her seat like a little kid. She said, "Okay. Let's do this!" She put up her hand and they all high-fived her around the table, giggling like fools.

Gabby could see the two women who had recognized her glancing sidelong to their table but she didn't really care. Now that she realized her identity was completely separate from the fantasy she had created with Evangeline, she wasn't so worried what people thought of her. She had such a feeling of rightness in her gut when she thought about Megan wearing that dress. Finally, the right bride would wear it. She was also excited about being a bridesmaid for the first time in her life. And as for Wade? She felt a little like Scarlett O'Hara at the end of Gone with the Wind. This wasn't over. Somehow, she was going to get him back.

Maybe it was knowing that he had finally said no to her but she suddenly realized why no other relationship had ever worked out. Wade was the love of her life. Yes, he could be demanding and he didn't always treat her like a princess. Sometimes, he could be stubborn and infuriating. But he was strong and decent, funny and sexy. And she'd been in love with him since she was nineteen years old. Terrified she'd screw it up and so she had screwed it up repeatedly.

The girls all decided to call their husbands or in Megan's

case, her fiancé. They invited her to stay but she had somewhere else she had to be and she didn't have much time.

As she was leaving, she said, "Megan, call me when you want to start thinking about dress designs. In fact, if you want all the girls to come, we can work something out that everybody likes."

They all looked at her in surprise. No wonder, she wasn't usually a design by committee type, but, for this particular wedding, she wanted each of them to have something they genuinely loved. If this was to be the end of her career, she wanted to go out with a bang.

CHAPTER 14

*S*he called Carlos and he picked her up in front of Señor Hooch. When he dropped her back at her house, she said, "Wait for me," and ran upstairs to her bedroom. She headed straight for her closet.

There were walk-in closets and walk-in closets. When Evangeline had bought this house she'd had the double closets extended into the second bedroom. It was like Aladdin's cave of fashion treasure in there. She had collected pieces that she had modeled, a few of the clothes she'd made for herself, and outfits that she just loved. She flipped on the lights and walked deeper and deeper. It was like going back in time.

She touched the gown she had worn when Peter was nominated for an Oscar one year. Perhaps she'd revealed a tad too much skin but the media had loved it.

Here was the gold lamé dress she had worn for her first ever cover shoot. This was from a Vogue cover. And then, she got to the dress she'd come in here for.

The white muslin was so simple Jane Austen might have worn it. In fact, she thought she'd been going through a Jane Austen phase when she and Wade had first become engaged.

She carried the dress carefully out into her bedroom and slipped it out of its garment bag. She hung it on the rack she used for her clothes when she was dressing and undressing This was the first wedding dress she had ever designed. And, it had the added charm that she had sewn it herself. Quickly she slipped off her gray dress once more, tossed it on the bed and slipped into the gown. This precursor to the Evangeline bridal empire didn't have a row of silk-covered buttons, it didn't boast a thousand real pearls hand sewn to the bodice. But that dress had been made with such love and such hope. She zipped up the back and to her satisfaction found that almost twenty years later, it still fit perfectly.

When she glanced at herself in the mirror she kept in her dressing room, she felt the way she had when she looked at Megan in the Evangeline gown. *This* was her dress. Now, all she needed was a groom.

Carefully, she removed her wedding dress and laid it on her bed. She brushed her hair, brushed her teeth, touched up her makeup and then, knowing that she was about to take the biggest risk of her life, she walked back into that closet. Back down the way she'd come, past where the wedding gown had hung. It took her a moment to find the dress she was searching for, but only a moment. She catalogued her clothes chronologically. And there it was. She thought she'd kept it. The black dress she had been wearing the first time she met Wade. Would he even remember? Probably not. But it meant something to her. She remembered trying to look older back then, or at least more sophisticated. She tried to rapidly recreate her hairstyle from that day. She'd worn her hair piled high, but in a messy, I-just-threw-this-together way. She ran to the bathroom and did throw a style together. She didn't still have the same shoes she'd worn—they'd been sky-high stilettos she could barely walk in. But she had plenty of black stilettos and she soon found a pair she liked.

Taking a deep breath, she slipped into that black dress that she had been wearing the moment her life changed forever. She very much hoped the dress would work its magic a second time. She checked the time and caught the double glitter of her engagement ring and the ruby and diamond bracelet. *Red lipstick*. She had worn red lipstick the night they met. She went back into her bathroom where she stocked red lipsticks in every possible shade. She chose a pomegranate color.

She didn't have time for more. She kept a small makeup kit with the essentials, plus a spare toothbrush, in her purse. She could fix herself up in the car.

The last thing she did was to take her wedding dress and fold it carefully into tissue paper and slip it into her large bag.

When she ran back down to where Carlos patiently waited, she threw herself into the back and told him to take her to Wade's hotel.

As they drove, she called Wade's cell phone. He didn't pick up. It. He had said he was leaving tonight, but she had no idea what time, or what airline. Could he be already on the plane? Was that why his cell phone was off? No. She shook her head. She refused to believe it.

She leaned forward, half wishing she'd taken her sports car. "Carlos, he's leaving tonight and I really need to get hold of him before he's gone."

"I'll do my best. I know a couple of shortcuts."

Carlos had hidden talents, she discovered, as her driver ducked into alleyways and tried to dodge the worst of the late afternoon traffic. When he drew up at the hotel she jumped out before the uniformed greeters reached the car.

She ran into the hotel. Realizing she was making a spectacle of herself, racing in a black cocktail dress and heels, she slowed, but not very much. She got to the reception desk. The young man who greeted her looked her up and down with an approving glance.

"Could you ring Wade Davenport's room please?"

"It would be my pleasure."

He tapped away on the computer for a moment while frustration boiled within her. *Come on, come on!* She needed to talk to Wade before he left. And then her stomach plummeted like an out-of-control elevator when he shook his head. "I'm sorry, ma'am. He checked out."

"He said he was flying out tonight. Do you know what flight he's catching?"

The young guy looked like he wanted to help her but he shook his head once more. "I'm sorry, ma'am. We're not allowed to give out information like that." She gave him her best smile. Flashed her engagement ring at him. "But I am his fiancée. His phone is off and I need to reach him urgently."

He gave her back the dazzling grin, and she suspected that he was moonlighting as a front desk clerk while waiting for his big break as the next Brad Pitt. "I wish I could help you."

"What time did he check out?"

A woman about her own age emerged from a door behind the front desk. The clerk turned to her. "Did you by any chance check out Wade Davenport? Suite 21B?"

The glance she gave Gabby suggested she knew perfectly well who Evangeline was but, as with so many hotels in LA, it was understood that not a flicker of recognition would be allowed to cross her face. There'd be no gushing, no asking for autographs; instead she said, "I believe I did help Mr. Davenport. How can I help you?"

When she explained the situation, the manager, whose name was Barbara, according to her badge, said, "It was about thirty minutes ago. He got us to print off his boarding pass. He's flying United. I believe the flight leaves at seven-thirty. You'd better hurry."

"Thanks, Barbara."

She jumped back into her car and told Carlos to race to LAX. "Wade's plane leaves at seven-thirty."

"At this time of night, it'll take over an hour to get there." He was already rolling. "But I'll get you there as fast as I can."

Her stomach was jumping with nerves and she kept pressing the floor in the back of the car as though she had a personal accelerator back here. She had to resist the urge to tell Carlos to go faster, move into the other lane. She knew she was being hysterical and she had to get herself under control, but she had this overwhelming feeling that if she didn't make things right today nothing would ever be the same again.

Traffic crawled along in typical LA-at-rush-hour fashion. The only consolation she had was that Wade could be no more than half an hour ahead of her according to the information she had received at the hotel and so his cab was probably stuck in the same traffic she was. The knowledge didn't help. She tried his cell again and got voicemail. Was his cell really turned off or was he avoiding her calls?

She dug into her bag and pulled out the red lipstick and even though her lips were still perfectly red, she added a little more color anyway. There was something about a red lipstick that gave a woman confidence. She stared out of the window. Then saw a commotion in the car beside her and realized that a middle aged couple had recognized her. They were waving. The husband tried to take a picture of her through the two vehicle windows. They were so cute. She waved back. And then finally traffic broke a little. Even so, she had nearly driven her finger-nails through her palms by the time they reached LAX. Her car screeched up to the entrance and she dashed out. As she was slamming the door, Carlos called out "Good luck!"

Oh and she was going to need it.

She ran forward. Found the check-in desk. "I'm looking for a passenger on the seven-thirty flight to New York. It's very important I talk to him." Why hadn't she done an Internet search in the car on the way here? At least she could have found the flight number, checked to see if the plane was maybe, hopefully, please, please, please, delayed.

The young woman glanced up and did the usual double take when a person spots a celebrity.

"It's my fiancé. Wade Davenport."

The woman nodded. "Right. I saw an interview with you two. I'm glad you worked it out. It gives a woman like me hope that, you know, even when you're not so young you can still find a great guy."

The trouble she seemed to be having was keeping that great guy. "So, can we get hold of him?"

She woman shook her head." Sorry. That flight is boarding."

"No. It can't be. I have to talk to him." She grabbed her bag. Pulled out her wallet. "Can I still buy a seat?"

"You'll have to run."

"I'll take anything in first-class."

She put an astonishing amount of money on her platinum card for a flight she didn't intend to take. She'd think about that later.

The woman handed over her ticket and said, "Go!"

She did. Sprinting in heels. She wasn't the greatest athlete in the world, but she thought she might have set a speed record for running in heels. She was panting when she got to security. After practically stripping naked, shoving all her belongings into a gray plastic bin that had seen better days, she walked through the electronic security gate and the beeping thing went off. The young security guy looked like she'd made his day. He said, "Stand with your arms out please."

She did as she was told, willing him to go faster. Please, let the plane not leave without her.

He ran the wand around her chest level and the wand bleated like it was oversexed. "It's my underwire bra," she told him in a low voice.

He nodded. "I know. We get that a lot." Still, he had to do his job, which she understood, even as every cell in her body vibrated with the urge to run. Then, finally, she was free to go. Of course, the plane was at the farthest possible departure gate. Instead of looking cool and collected, by the time she got to the gate she was sweating like a pig, her ankles bent over like a crippled person's because she hadn't put her shoes back on properly and she was heaving like a steam engine. She burst into the departure lounge. There were only three people still lining up to get on the plane. Three people. And not one of them was Wade.

At least the plane hadn't left. She joined the short line. When it was her turn, she presented her ticket and said, "Can you confirm for me that a passenger is on board this plane? He's my fiancé."

She was greeted with yet another head shake. "Sorry. Security regulations."

Here she was, about to board a flight to New York without even a change of underwear. She had a twenty-year-old wedding dress with her, never worn, but not so much as a clean pair of panties. And she had no idea if the man she was pursuing was even on the damn plane.

But, she had a credit card. And she'd found in her life that as long as she had some cash and a credit card, there wasn't much she couldn't get. She tried to catch her breath as she headed to the plane.

She was hopping on one foot waiting for the person in front of her to board when a voice behind her said, "Gabby?"

She turned and there was Wade, striding towards her. She felt her smile bloom and relief clutch at her chest. "You're not on the plane."

"No. Traffic was terrible. Plus, I got here and there's like fifteen missed calls from you so I was worried. I was trying to call you back. Your phone's off."

She snorted with nervous laughter. "No, the battery ran down."

He looked at her, clearly realizing that she wasn't here by coincidence.

"Wade. I need to talk to you. I couldn't let you leave without telling you, I love you."

"And you wait until we're in the jet bridge to tell me? I have to get on this plane. I really do have important business in New York."

She didn't know what she'd expected when she declared her love, but more than to hear his agenda! She didn't have a speech prepared. She'd pretty much thought those three little words would fix everything. Seemed she was wrong. "I know. I bought a ticket so I could tell you."

He shook his head. "Have I ever told you that you are completely crazy?"

Her lips twitched at that. "I think you first told me that when I was nineteen years old."

"So it's not a new problem."

She shook her head. "Also, probably incurable."

For all the rushing to get here, there was some kind of holdup and a short line of people still waited to board. She said, "I'm sorry. That was the other important thing I had to tell you." Then she realized she had to explain her crazed race to the airport. "I went to the bar with those girls. No, wait. First I tried that dress on. It looked like crap on me. That dress was meant for Megan O'Reilly." She shook her head. "You were right about everything. I was never going to wear that dress. It was wrong of me to make up that story about being engaged to you. It was wrong of me to manipulate you like that. And I'm sorry." She glanced down at the beautiful ring she'd enjoyed wearing for the past few weeks. She slid the ring off with shaky hands and offered it to Wade. When he held out his palm and let her drop the ring into it, the mist in front of her eyes deepened to a lake. "I'm sorry," she said again.

He closed his hand over the ring and she was grateful, not that anyone was paying them any attention, but she didn't want the whole world to know that she'd just got unengaged. "But if you let Megan wear that dress and we don't continue with the fiction that we are engaged, what happens to your business?"

She shrugged. "I don't know. Maybe that nasty journalist will keep trying to convince people that my business is cursed. Maybe it is. But it doesn't matter. If I don't design wedding gowns I'll figure out something else to do. In fact, I have an idea. I got it when I was drinking margaritas with those brides, at Señor Hooch if you can believe it. I realized that every woman should get to wear a dress that makes her feel like a princess. I might look into taking some of my more successful gowns and putting out an everyday line. Not obviously with the finest silk and real pearls but with the same style as the original. The kind of dress I could afford when I was young."

"Wow. I don't know what they put in the margaritas at Señor Hooch but you've come a long way in a couple of hours."

They got to the edge of the plane. He stepped on but she hung back. There was no point flying to New York. She'd said what she had come to say.

He'd taken back the ring.

Wade glanced back. "Are you coming?"

His expression made her ask, "I don't know. Should I?"

He held out his hand. "You definitely should."

She took his hand and they walked onto the plane. Of course, their seats were rows apart, but Wade used his charm and maybe her celebrity status helped. Someone offered to move and soon they were sitting side-by-side.

Wade leaned close. "I know we have a lot to talk about, but could we go back to the *you love me* part?"

She imagined this was what it must feel like for a skydiver to stand on the edge of the plane and look down at the earth rushing by so far below, to take that step out into the unknown and let go of the last vestiges of security, not knowing if your parachute was going to open or not. She took a deep breath. And then took the plunge. "I don't think I've ever loved anyone else. That's why none of my relationships ever worked."

She tried to be honest so she added, "Well, that and being high maintenance and demanding. But, I was too scared. I was too scared and I screwed up. But when I stupidly claimed I was getting married, your name was the only one I thought of. And you came. Because I asked you to. And these past weeks have been, well, magic."

"So, what are you saying, exactly?"

He would not make this easier for her. "I think I'm saying, will you marry me? For real this time."

"If I say yes, will you snatch that gown back from the poor girl who wants it so much?"

"No. That dress is hers. I have a very different gown in mind for my wedding."

He sat there for a moment. He seemed to be considering her proposal as though it were a merger he might have to take a gamble on. She felt so nervous she wanted to start listing her good points. Try to sell him on her as a bride. Finally, he said, "No. I decline your very flattering offer."

And there it was. The parachute that wouldn't open. She felt the hard ground rushing towards her and she was incapable of stopping the crash. Then he spoke again, "I think I'm surprisingly old-fashioned about some things. I always thought the man should do the proposing."

"Oh." Maybe her parachute was going to open after all. She stared at him. "Are you planning to propose any time soon?"

"Could you give me a moment?"

"I'm nervous."

He took a breath. "For a man who's had enough practice

proposing to you, you'd think I'd get it right by now. It should be done somewhere romantic like on top of the Eiffel Tower or something."

She shook her head. "No. This is very romantic. This is the most romantic place I've ever been."

He chuckled. "I am not getting on my knee in a crowded plane that is about to take off."

"Okay."

He leaned over and took her hand. "Gabby Brock", then he had to speak up because the engines began to roar. "I love you and I want to spend the rest of my life with you. I love your beauty and your intelligence and your creativity. I even like your temper. At least you're not dull. And you never leave a man in doubt about what you're thinking. Will you marry me?"

"Oh, Wade." She threw her arms around him and he kissed her hungrily. Then he took her left hand. And he slipped the engagement ring back where it belonged.

The flight attendant came along with a tray containing glasses of champagne, some glasses of water, and a couple of orange juice. "Would you care for a drink before takeoff?"

She laughed. "I think a glass of champagne would be perfect." She took two glasses off the tray and passed one to her very brand-new fiancé.

They clicked glasses. "To us," he said.

CHAPTER 15

ade had a car and driver waiting for him at LaGuardia and they were soon whisked to his townhouse in the Upper East Side. In the wee hours of the morning New York was as quiet as it ever got. Cabs rolled along, the odd emergency vehicle screamed by.

Even though they usually got together for lunch or a drink when she was in his city or he in hers, she'd never been inside his home. He'd long ago upgraded from the tiny apartment he'd owned two decades ago.

The interior of his home was ultra modern and sleek. The walls and furniture were all in neutral shades as though the whole place were an elaborate frame for the wild bursts of color in the paintings. "I see you collect art." She hadn't known he had an interest in emerging artists. Sadness washed over her that they'd let so much time go by.

He kissed her. "I keep my best pieces in my bedroom."

She laughed at him even as desire curled in her belly. "I'm not a bit surprised."

121

SHE WOKE at what seemed like the middle of the night to find Wade dressed and putting on his shoes. She blinked sleepily. "What time is it?"

"Seven. Go back to sleep."

They hadn't arrived until after three, then they'd made love. She imagined if he'd slept at all, it had been for minutes. "I wish you didn't have to go," she mumbled.

"I wish I did not have to go to this meeting, but I really do. I'll leave you my driver's number. He'll take you anywhere you want to go today."

He leaned over and kissed her.

"You trust me all alone in your place? You don't think I'll snoop?"

"We're getting married. Go ahead and snoop. You should know my secrets." The way he said those words sent a shiver down her spine. What was nice about rekindling the romance was discovering that he did have secrets and it was fun to explore them.

"I'll call you."

He kissed her again and then he was gone.

She rolled over, found herself on his side of the bed, and snuggled against his pillow.

WADE COULD BARELY CONCENTRATE on his meeting. He felt foolishly out of his head as he tried to focus on incomes and outflows and merger possibilities when all he really cared about was getting back to Gabby. That woman had been turning him inside out for the better part of two decades. He couldn't wait to see what she had in store for him for the next few.

"You find our proposal amusing?" Kurt Heise asked him in perfect English.

The sarcastic comment pulled him back to the meeting. "No. Sorry. I was thinking of something else."

Strangely, perhaps because the German businessmen could see he wasn't particularly invested in the negotiations, they went his way more. They presented their proposals in the morning, had lunch catered in the boardroom and then in the afternoon the serious negotiating began. The four men from the German team and his people shook hands at the end of the meeting. In all business dealings Wade tried to make sure everyone walked away from the table, if not perfectly happy, at least with mutual respect and integrity intact. He felt that had happened when he left the office after bidding his guests goodbye.

He got in the car and called Gabby.

She answered right away. "Hello, husband-to-be," she said in her sexy British accent.

"Hello, yourself." He couldn't help the grin that spread over his face. How did he ever get so lucky? Not so many hours ago he'd packed his bag and felt as though in leaving LA he was leaving his heart behind. Now, he was engaged to the greatest woman in all the world. "I thought we'd have dinner somewhere. I don't know what your favorite places are anymore." And he would have to change that very soon. He wanted to know everything about her. All her newest chosen restaurants, because Gabby had very definite taste and she was usually right. She would get enthusiastic about everything from the best flower shop to the best coffee shop. Simply being out on the town with her was an adventure.

Her answer surprised him. "Come home. We're eating in."

A lot of things about Gabby Brock had changed, but if she'd suddenly learned how to cook, this was the first he'd heard about it. Frankly, he didn't care. He liked everything about being alone with her for one evening.

He had his driver pull over to a corner store with buckets of flowers displayed on the pavement outside. He grabbed an arrangement of daisies, roses, and something that smelled like perfume.

When he got to his townhouse he couldn't wait to get inside the door and see her. He'd missed her so much today he felt foolish at his own craving. Even though he owned the place he knocked first and then used his key.

From the small foyer he could see the flicker of candlelight coming from the living room. When he drew closer he saw she'd also put on the gas fireplace. It was July and she'd put on the fire. It wasn't the sticky heat of late summer, but it was still a warm summer evening. Dinner, it seemed, was a picnic on the floor. He had a nice rooftop terrace, but he knew exactly why she'd chosen this picnic spot.

A bottle of champagne chilled in an ice bucket and on the floor was a series of paper cartons. She wore the same black dress she'd worn to meet him yesterday, but her feet were bare. He walked up to her, kissed her long and lovingly. "I've been thinking about that all day," he admitted. Then he gestured to the paper containers. "Don't tell me you found our old favorite Chinese place?"

"Of course I did. I think it's now the son and his wife running it but hopefully they're still using the same family recipes."

"You look good in my living room."

"That's fantastic news because I intend to spend a lot of time here in the future."

He ran a finger around the neckline of her dress. "I like that dress very much."

She said with a quizzical look, "Do you?" He could tell she was waiting to see if he recognized it.

"I do. It reminds me of this gorgeous young girl I once saw across a crowded room at a London party. She was wearing a dress just like this."

She tilted her head. "Did she look as good in it is I do?"

He shook his head. "No one could look as good in that dress as you do."

She laughed. "That was exactly the right thing to say."

"I can't believe you still have it."

She traced the buttons of his shirt as though she were counting them. "I always save the clothes that are really special to me. Walking into my closet is a bit like going through an old photo album. This was always one of my favorites."

He took the flowers from her and laid them on the table. Later, they'd put them in water. Later.

"Do you want a glass of champagne?" she asked him.

He kissed her right where her shoulder met her neck and she shivered. "No."

"Do you want some dinner?"

She must know the answer to that, since he had her zipper halfway down her back. "No."

"You're a difficult man to please." She already sounded breathless and turned on.

"Not when you're around."

The dress slid to the floor like a shadow of the past. She stepped out of it and he nearly swallowed his tongue.

Her underwear was, he was fairly certain, from her own high-end line of lingerie. If there was any body Evangeline knew how to design for it was that of Gabby Brock. The set was silk and café-au-lait colored. Even though he didn't know much about women's lingerie he knew perfectly well that the silk was real and that lace was probably French and worth a fortune. It wasn't what she'd been wearing last night. Sometime today she'd gone shopping.

He needed it off and now. He kissed her, pulled her into his arms, and let all the pent-up longing out. She made a sound in the back of her throat almost like a growl and suddenly his suit jacket was on the floor. His shirt soon followed. Together they fumbled out of their clothes with more haste than style.

Her limbs were long and slender. He'd always loved her height and the way they fit so well together. As a very tall man, it was nice for him to find a woman who reached higher than his shoulder. She'd always claimed her arms and legs were freakishly long, but he liked them that way. Maybe she had to have her clothes custom made but her height and long limbs were partly what had made her so successful as a model. He wasn't so concerned about that part, he loved the way they fit together and the way those long arms and legs could wrap around him. They made love in front of the gas fireplace too desperate for each other to make it to the bedroom. When he looked deep into her eyes as they were joined in the most intimate way, his heart rejoiced. The woman looking back was all Gabby.

He didn't mind the flash and polish and celebrity of Evangeline, though in truth he preferred a more quiet, anonymous life, but he understood that life with a celebrity was always going to have certain challenges. However, when it was just the two of them, it was Gabby he wanted. She'd always been full of challenges and that was part of what he loved about her.

Much later, once they were wrapped in soft bathrobes, a navy one for him and a cranberry colored one for her, they sat on the floor eating the Chinese food and drinking champagne. He leaned forward and traced the V of her robe, where it gaped. "I like you in this."

"You'd better get used to seeing me in it. When I set off to find you yesterday I didn't intend to fly several thousand miles and end up in New York. I brought absolutely nothing with me. Well, except one thing."

She got to her feet and retrieved her large handbag from the couch. She opened it and pulled out something white and folded carefully. It looked like a white nightgown. Who travelled with a nightgown when they weren't even planning to spend the night away from home? And then she glanced at him shyly and shook out the garment. "I can't try this on for you, because everyone knows it's bad luck for the groom to see his bride in her wedding gown before the wedding. And heaven knows we've had enough bad luck."

He stared at the white gown. It was slightly wrinkled, but gauzy and romantic. "You're going to have to explain this to me. That doesn't look like one of your Evangeline designer gowns to me."

She looked at the dress, looked at him and suddenly laughed. "In fact, it is. This is the very first wedding dress I ever designed. I also sewed it myself, which I no longer do. It wasn't made with as much expertise as I have these days but I've never put so much love into a single garment."

He got to his feet and strode over to her. He touched the gauzy fabric. He felt emotion well in him. "You've had that gown all this time? When did you make it?"

"The first time we got engaged. I finished it probably two days before I panicked and ran away. I wasn't very mature and I certainly wasn't in touch with my own feelings. But, I hope the dress proves one thing. I absolutely did intend to marry you." She gazed up at him from under her thick lashes and those deep blue eyes knocked him out as they always did. "I still intend to wear it when I marry you."

The more she said those words the more he began to believe that this time they might actually pull off a wedding. But he had a hard time believing she'd wear that gown down the aisle. "What are the fine people at *Cheerio!* Magazine going to say when the great Evangeline turns up at her wedding in a dress hand sewn by a nineteen-year-old with simple, inexpensive fabric?"

She leaned in and lowered her voice as though she were letting him in on a great secret. "The people at *Cheerio!* Magazine won't be at our wedding. In fact, after all this curse business and the focus on me and my business, I don't want my wedding to be a media circus or a calculated way of proving to the world that Evangeline and her business are not cursed. It doesn't matter. What matters is that this is our life and our wedding and I want it to be small and perfect. Also, as private as possible."

He scratched his nose. "Life never seems to go the way you imagine it will does it? Well, you've got the dress. Why don't we get married at City Hall?"

She nodded enthusiastically. "Yes. That's a fantastic idea. When?"

"As soon as is humanly possible." He pulled her against him, crushing the dress between them and kissing the life out of her. "I have loved you and I've let you go too many times. I warn you now, this time I am not letting you go without a fight."

She sighed and put her head on his shoulder. "This time, I'm not running away. I'm not running anymore."

He'd marry her tomorrow if he could, but he didn't want her to rush into anything she'd regret. "What about family and friends?"

"We should allow our friends and families to help us celebrate. But there is no way to do that without a huge production that I don't want. This isn't Evangeline getting married, Wade. This is Gabby Brock and I want to have a Gabby Brock wedding."

"I tell you what, we'll get married as soon as we can, only the two of us, and then throw a big party in LA to celebrate. We can throw one here, too, if you like, and maybe one in London."

She nodded. "The parties will be for everyone else, but our wedding is just for us." She sighed against him. "Can we really get married tomorrow?"

He shrugged. "I don't know. Let's look online." He opened his laptop and tapped away for a few minutes.

Gabby loved the competent way he did things. Each task seemed to have his full attention, whether it was making love to her or researching City Hall marriages online. She knew she was badly, deeply in love when she found herself watching his strong fingers tapping on the keyboard. She loved his hands. In fact, there wasn't much of him she didn't love. He glanced up as though feeling her eyes on him. "It looks pretty easy. We fill out the paperwork online and we both have to take it down to City Hall to get a marriage license. Then we have to wait twenty-four hours before we can get married. Which means we can get married the day after tomorrow."

Unfamiliar nerves jumbled around in her stomach. He was reaching a hand to her and it was up to her to take it. She nodded. "Let's do it."

She settled beside him and they filled out the online form together. Then she asked, "What time are the appointments? I hope we can still get a good time."

He shook his head. "No appointments. The marriage office opens at eight-thirty in the morning and you can show up anytime before three-forty-five and take a number. Then you wait until they call you. It says on this website it can take up to three hours."

"Three hours of waiting at City Hall to get married?" She shook her head. "Really, Wade, I'm sure I can pull a few strings and get us a proper appointment."

His eyes twinkled. "Maybe Evangeline could. How many strings can Gabby Brock pull?"

She started to splutter and scheme, but then realized he was right. Part of the adventure was getting married simply as Gabby and Wade not as a top financier and a somewhat tarnished celebrity. "Oh all right. I suggest we get there at eight-thirty then so at least we won't have to wait too long."

"We'll take the paperwork in tomorrow and get married the day after."

She nodded. "That's probably better. I need to do some shopping. I'll need shoes." And a wedding ring for Wade.

Eight-thirty was a ridiculously early hour to get married. But she didn't care. She'd never been so happy in all her life.

The only moment when it seemed that their perfect happiness was going to be marred was when she explained to Wade that she would be spending the night before the wedding at the Waldorf. He was completely baffled. "What? I finally got you back in my life and already you're taking off to a hotel?"

She put her arms around him. "I don't want to leave you even for one second. But, once a woman's been cursed, it's amazing how she becomes a little more superstitious. It's bad luck for you to see me wear my wedding gown before the wedding, and I don't want any bad luck with us. I'm spending the night at the hotel and I'll get a car to drive me to the courthouse. I will meet you there."

He put a hand to his forehead as though checking for fever. "All right."

He printed off the marriage form. "When do you need to be back in LA?"

"I've got a laptop with me. My phone. And a wonderful staff." She grinned at him. "Make that team. I don't have anything that can't be postponed, until next Wednesday. That's when Megan O'Reilly and her bridesmaids are meeting. I've got to sketch out some design ideas for bridesmaid dresses, but I can do that here. I don't want to postpone that meeting, though. Those girls are special."

"Okay."

"Why? Do you want me out of the way?"

"Never. I have a surprise for you."

She kissed him. "I love surprises." Then she kissed him again. "And I love you."

CHAPTER 16

*G*abby woke on her wedding day with a sense of anticipation she hadn't felt in years. She had that wonderful feeling in between sleeping and waking that something amazing was going to happen to her and she couldn't wait to open her eyes and jump out of bed and find out exactly what it was going to be.

And then she woke fully and saw her freshly pressed wedding dress hanging in the hotel closet. She'd left the doors open so that she'd be able to see it before she went to sleep last night. All alone in her big bed in the hotel. Maybe she was being silly, but it wasn't only superstition that had her sleeping apart from Wade on the night before their wedding. She savored every moment that she missed him and knew that soon they'd share a bed every night.

She felt old-fashioned and romantic. She dressed with care, putting on some of the new silk underwear she'd purchased the day before. It was Evangeline, naturally, and even she was shocked at how pricey the stuff was in retail. But the silk was luxurious against her skin. Since she had so few cosmetics with her, she kept her makeup light, which suited the simple dress.

She wore her hair long, but she did use her connections to get a very early hair appointment, so her curls shone.

When she reached the courthouse on Fourth she found her knees were shaking. She hadn't been this nervous since her first runway show. The driver opened the door for her and she stepped out, clutching a tiny handbag. "Thank you," she said. She paid him his fee, plus gave him a generous tip. On this day, everyone should have something to be happy about. Then she turned to where her new life waited for her.

She glanced up and Wade was walking toward her. He wore a gray suit and he'd had his hair trimmed. He was holding a bouquet of white roses. When he reached her, she thought he might make a joke about her actually showing up, but he said, "You look beautiful."

He handed her the roses.

"Oh how beautiful. White roses were the first flowers you ever bought me."

"I have better taste and more imagination now, but I went with nostalgia."

"These are perfect." She took one of the long-stemmed roses and snapped it, then tucked the single rose into his buttonhole. "Are you ready?"

"I've been ready for almost twenty years."

They walked in holding hands and found there was a couple already ahead of them. A young Latino couple. The girl wore a short organdy wedding dress and the groom wore a suit with the discomfort of a man who rarely wears one. They walked up to the counter, gave their names and were given a number. They were sent to sit on a padded bench upholstered in green vinyl while they waited. The other groom didn't seem to know what to do with his hands. He tapped the bench beside him, then his fiancée's leg, then he folded his hands and jiggled them up and down between his knees. He looked up, nodded. "Big day."

"Sure is," Wade said. Then he smiled at the couple. "Congratulations."

"Thanks. You too."

She was suddenly filled with affection for this young couple. She thought she might think of them every year when she and Wade celebrated their wedding anniversary.

The young woman kept glancing towards the door. "Where are they?"

"They'll be here," her groom promised without much conviction.

"If they blow us off, who's going to witness our marriage?"

She and Wade looked at each other. Witnesses? They needed witnesses? Somehow they'd missed that bit of information when they'd prepared for today.

They both knew people in New York they could call but the whole point of this event was for it to be only the two of them.

The other couple's number was called. At the same time, two other couples came in together.

The young woman said, "I hate to ask you guys, but would you be our witnesses?"

Her affection for the sweet young couple grew. "Of course. We didn't even know we needed witnesses—could you do the same for us?"

"Yeah. Absolutely."

And so the four of them headed into the chapel. It was badly named since it was basically a boring square room. However, the officiant was a cheerful man with dark hair and a mustache who seemed to love his work. He didn't blink when they explained they would be the witnesses for each other. "Efficient," he said. "I like that."

The young man handed Wade a camera. "Do you mind? Our friends were supposed to take pictures."

"Not at all."

And so, Gabby and Wade witnessed Pilar and Herrando's

marriage and Wade was the official photographer. She still felt emotion well up inside her even though the ceremony was short and she was watching people she didn't even know. She felt hope for this couple, so filled with happiness and confidence for the future, hope for her and Wade, who'd had to wait so long to find each other again. When the officiant proclaimed them married, the young man took his bride into his arms and kissed her hard.

And then she and Wade were the ones getting married. In all her dreams of this day—and she'd had plenty of them over the years—she had never imagined herself being married in New York at City Hall. But it was so simple. She didn't have to worry about looking her best, worry about what pictures would be leaked to the media. Instead of hand picking the photographers who'd be allowed in, she had an amateur snapping photos with Wade's cell phone.

She didn't need to feel that she was representing the Evangeline brand. She didn't have to worry about anything except enjoying this moment and this man and finally wearing this dress that she had sewn herself with such love so many years ago. When the four of them were walking out, Pilar said to Gabby, "I hope you don't mind me saying this, but you look exactly like someone famous. I can't place it."

Gabby smiled at her. "I get that a lot."

Once they were back out front, the young couple's friends arrived with balloons and flowers and many apologies for being late. They said they hadn't been able to get a babysitter in time.

Wade shook hands with Hernando and Gabby hugged Pilar. "Good luck," she said. And she really meant it.

He pulled out his cell phone and scrolled through the pictures, holding the camera so she could see too.

Gabby had been photographed by top photographers all over the world. She'd been airbrushed and retouched and paid a fortune for her image. And here she was, on the most important day of her life, checking her wedding photos on a cell phone. The notion made her ridiculously happy.

They passed three more couples on their way to be married. And then they were outside, and Wade's car swooped over to pick them up.

Wade opened the back door and she got in. A picnic basket sat on the seat of the limousine which drove them to Central Park. Wade popped the bottle of champagne that was cooling and poured two glasses. "To my beautiful bride."

She leaned forward and kissed him softly. "To us."

Inside the picnic hamper were tiny quiches and croissants and fresh fruit and cheese, which they ate while they drove. She'd assumed that they would get out and walk around the park or something but the driver didn't stop. "Where are we going?"

"That's your surprise. We're going on our honeymoon."

Her eyebrows rose. "Our honeymoon? I don't have any clothes!"

His glance was deliciously wicked. "It's your honeymoon. You will not need clothes."

Gabby, a woman who had worked so hard to control her life and her image and her business, laughed with delight and sat back. She had no idea where they were going, but she imagined a woman with a credit card could find the essentials. And Wade was right. She didn't imagine she would have any immediate need for clothes.

When they pulled into a private airfield, she said, "You chartered a plane?"

"My company owns it."

"And it's taking us where?"

"A very nice resort in the Bahamas. I know you have to be back on Wednesday so we're only staying four days. We'll take a proper honeymoon later. There are so many places I want to show you."

She knew exactly how he felt. She wanted to show him all her special places, too, and imagined they would make plenty of new memories. "And I you."

When Gabby returned to her office in Los Angeles she was lightly tanned, relaxed in body and spirit and filled to brimming with optimism.

"Isn't it a beautiful day?" she asked the receptionist as she strode into the doors of Evangeline design. The young woman nodded nervously. "Yes ma'am. It is."

Gabby laughed and placed one of the daisies she had picked from her own garden this morning and laid it on the girl's desk. "Cheer up. Things can't be that bad."

Her good mood continued until she got to the reception area outside her own studio where Salvador ran the everyday operations.

He glanced up at her and while he got to his feet, kissed her on both cheeks and told her she looked sublime, she could see he was only going through the motions.

"Why the long faces around here?" she asked.

"Eve, we have to talk."

She knew in the deepest part of herself that nothing was so very bad that it couldn't be fixed. She said, "Come on through."

"You haven't seen the papers?" In his hands he held one of those horrible tabloid rags.

She felt the tiniest simmer of temper. Could those wretched sewer rats not find someone else to destroy? Then realized that it didn't matter. She said, "Oh my goodness, what are they up to now?"

She held her hands out for the paper and Salvador scanned her desktop before handing it over. He said, "Is there anything sharp or deadly I should worry about?"

"Oh, honestly, it was only that one time. And I wasn't aiming at you. I was aiming for the wall."

"You've got a very bad aim when you're angry." He rubbed his shoulder in memory.

"I promise not to be angry."

She took the paper and spread it out in front of her and perused the article Salvador had highlighted. "Well, at least they spelled my name right."

Naturally, the byline on the article was Wolf Dixon, the man who seemed to have made it his personal mission to make her life miserable. But, what Wolf Dixon did not know was that she had an impenetrable barrier surrounding her. She'd married the man of her dreams, she was in love, and this sad little man was not going to ruin that.

The headline screamed, "Cursed Dress Designer Dumped by Fiancé."

The main photograph had been taken at Señor Hooch and showed her sipping her margarita. The second photograph showed her running like a madwoman through the lobby of the hotel where Wade had been staying. She skimmed the first few paragraphs of the article and began to laugh.

Salvador took a step towards the doorway. "Should I call somebody? You need coffee? Water? A tranquilizer? Your therapist?"

"No, none of those things. Oh, that poor ridiculous man."

She had no idea how much Wolf Dixon had been fed by various people who may have seen her crazed flight after Wade or overheard snatches of her conversations. Maybe the desk clerk waiting for his big acting break had made a few extra bucks. Someone at Señor Hooch clearly had. It didn't matter. Dixon had cobbled together a story about her being dumped by her fiancé, then getting embarrassingly drunk, though, fine journalist that he was, he'd preferred the term 'trashed' and then running like a crazy person after the man who'd dumped her.

Salvador said, "Well?"

"Apart from two grammatical errors and a couple of typos, it reads quite well. All garbage, of course."

"Three more brides cancelled their orders this morning."

"Good," she said briskly. "That gives me more time for the bridesmaid dresses I'm designing." She pulled out her initial sketches. "Can you get these transferred to computer? I want a quick turnaround on these dresses. Oh, and get my PR consultant on the phone. I want to have a press conference."

Before he left she stopped him. "Salvador, darling, I have to ask. Who's behind the leaks?"

His steps faltered. He turned. "You don't think it's me, do you?"

"No. Of course not. I've had a clearer head in the past few days and I did wonder if it was you. But we've been together a long time. I trust you. But I think you know who's been leaking information too." Salvador was smart, and in touch with the staff in a way she wasn't.

He didn't deny. He came back and sat down across from her. "I might be able to make an educated guess. What are you going to do?"

The old Gabby would have fired the person on the spot, but she was discovering a softer side. "I suppose it will depend on why they did it."

"Because they are still friends. She and Emise stayed in contact. I don't think she realized she was being pumped for information."

Emise was the woman who had cursed her. "Of course. How could I have been so stupid? It's the other seamstress who was there that day. Sonja, isn't it?"

Salvador didn't say anything. He didn't have to.

"Send for her. Tell her we both want to see her in my office, now."

He didn't move. "Eve. I beg of you, don't do anything rash.

We have a human resources department. We can work something out that leaves you untouchable."

She shook her head. "No. I would like to speak to her." She smiled at him. "Don't worry."

When Sonja entered the studio she appeared both frightened and defiant. Gabby didn't like disloyalty, but she had an odd sympathy for this girl. She'd been loyal to her friend, if not her employer. "Sit down," she said.

Salvador motioned her to a chair and took the second one himself.

There was a moment's silence. She said, "I'm not going to ask you if you've been leaking confidential information that has been used in negative media reports. What I am going to say is that I am sorry."

Both Sonja and Salvador stared at her with similar expressions of shock on their faces.

"I'm sorry I didn't handle myself better when Emise made that mistake. If you're in contact, I hope you will express my feelings to your friend. However, Evangeline is a team. We need to act as a team."

No one said anything so she continued. "I'm offering you two choices. If you're happy here, you are welcome to stay. I'm making some changes to the business model and there will be greater opportunities. Naturally, I will expect that no more confidential information gets leaked. If you'd like to leave, I can arrange a similar position with another designer. The job is in children's wear."

"There's an actual job?" Salvador asked.

"Of course there is."

Sonja's face grew bright red and then pale.

"You can think about it if you like."

"No." The young seamstress spoke at last. "I'd like to stay."

"Very well. There'll be no more said about it."

Sonja rose stiffly. When she got to the door, she turned and said, "Thank you."

Salvador waited until she was gone, then said, "Where were you? At an ashram or something?"

She chuckled. "So much better. I was on my honeymoon."

Salvador stood and said, "Come here." He kissed her on both cheeks and then hugged her. "Congratulations!"

When he left, she put the ridiculous article out of her head and got to work.

Wade texted her in the middle of the morning. "I miss you."

And he'd attached a photo from their honeymoon of the two of them on a sailboat he'd chartered. Luckily Gabby had managed to find the essentials she needed in the clothing shops at the stunningly beautiful resort. These included two brand-new bikinis, a pair of casual sandals, a colorful sarong wrap and a big floppy hat to keep off the sun. She'd also bought a couple of very casual beach dresses for dinners and their one excursion into town.

She and her brand new husband had made love and sailed and snorkeled, they'd eaten wonderful meals. And they had talked. Endlessly, it seemed, of everything they'd stored up for the last twenty years. They'd talked about the future and how they'd make it all work. She'd found time to sketch out a few of her ideas for the bridesmaid dresses.

She'd been inspired by the intense colors of the water and the tropical fish. She'd felt her creativity bloom and could hardly keep up with all her ideas. Marriage seemed to agree with her.

Later in the morning, needing a break, she walked down a floor to the couture area and consulted with her design team on fabrics and colors. She wanted to have a full presentation when Megan and her fellow bridesmaids arrived at four in the afternoon. She also had a few other tasks to take care of. The atmosphere was warmer than usual. She had a feeling that her uncharacteristically diplomatic handling of Sonja had somehow become known.

When Sarah, her PR consultant called she said, "Sarah, how lovely to hear from you," forgetting that she was the one who had asked Sarah to call her.

There was a tiny pause. "You sound surprisingly cheerful for someone whose fiancé dumped them and then they got drunk and chased after him."

"At least I was wearing a very pretty dress when I went chasing after Wade. If one's going to have one's picture plastered all over the cover of a tabloid newspaper, one at least likes to look one's best."

Sarah didn't seem in the mood for jokes. "You want the good news or the bad news?"

"I'm in the mood for good news."

In fact, she didn't believe any news today could be bad news. She was too happy. "Our investigator was able to track down Emise, your seamstress."

"That's the good news?"

"It is good news. She happily took the money, which of course we called severance pay, and then signed a nondisclosure agreement."

Gabby tried to be philosophical. The woman had done her a favor in a strange way. If it hadn't been for that curse she never would have foolishly announced to the world that she was engaged to Wade. She wouldn't currently be wearing his ring and her name would not be Gabrielle Brock Davenport. "And here's the funny thing," Sarah continued. "After she took the cash and signed the nondisclosure agreement she told our investigator that she's not a Gypsy. She's Hungarian. And she doesn't know any curses. Apparently, what she muttered were the words to the first verse of the Hungarian National Anthem."

For the second time that day Gabby broke into a peal of laughter. There was nothing musical or delicious about this laughter. It was a throaty, horsey laugh. Her eyes were streaming when she finally got herself under control. "I've been feng shui'd, I've been smudged, had my future predicted by Tarot cards and Lord knows what else. And there never was any curse?"

"There never was any curse. Now, about the press conference. There are a few ways we can do damage control. I have to ask, is there any truth at all to this rumor that you have a drinking problem?"

She chuckled once more. "Let me just say that I have never before set foot inside Señor Hooch and, as much as I enjoyed my single margarita, I don't make a habit of drinking to excess."

She could hear the relief in Sarah's tone. "Good. Is there any other falsehood in Wolf Dixon's article? Which, I'm sure you know, has been picked up all over the place online."

"I wouldn't expect anything else. There is one other tiny falsehood in the article. Wade and I did not break up. In fact, he will be with me at the press conference."

"Good. That's good. You two appearing together will go a long way to improving public perception. But, it would be fantastic if you could use that press conference to set a date for your wedding."

Oh this was just too much fun. She sat back and put her feet up on her desk, something she almost never did. She said, "I'm afraid that's impossible."

Sarah put on her tough voice. "Do we really have to go over this again?"

"We can't set the date because Wade and I were married quietly in a private ceremony in New York six days ago."

CHAPTER 17

*T*here was silence for a moment. She had the pleasure of knowing she had rendered her communications expert silent. "Wow! Congratulations. So that's what you're announcing?"

"Yes. And I'll also be releasing an official photograph or two of the ceremony."

"Fantastic. I'll get my staff onto the press conference right away. Where do you want to have it? At your home?"

"No. My husband is not a media personality and he prefers to keep our home life private. We'll have the media conference here at Evangeline. I will have a business-related announcement too."

For her first day back at work, she couldn't believe how much she was getting done.

At four o'clock, when Megan, Tasmine, Ashley, and Kate once more assembled in her studio she said, "There is so much I want to tell you girls I don't know where to start." She felt suddenly that these were her closest girlfriends, even though she barely knew any of them.

The women all looked slightly anxious. And she saw the

glances they cast each other when she welcomed them warmly and gave each of them a hug. Finally, Ashley said, "Evangeline, you know we didn't have anything to do with that awful newspaper report, right? In fact, we'll all go public and make statements if you'd like us to, saying that you only drank one margarita and none of us have ever seen you drunk."

She beamed at them. She'd been right. These were her kind of women. "That is so lovely of you. Thank you. Of course I know it wasn't you. When you live in the public eye, especially now, in the age of smart phones and Twitter and Instagram and the rest of it, you become a target." She pulled a bottle of Crystal champagne from her fridge. "If I let myself worry about every foolish article or unflattering photograph of me I'd go mad. Anyway, I'm having a press conference next week and I'd like you all to be there. Mostly, I want you there as my friends. And, as I feel like you are becoming my friends, I wanted to tell you the news." And then she squealed like a teenager seeing her favorite rock band and held out her left hand where her stunning engagement ring now sat cuddled up to its matching wedding band.

Megan was the first to recover. "You got married! Congratulations!" And she ran forward and threw her arms around Gabby impulsively. They all began talking at once, offering congratulations and asking for the story, and while they did Salvador slipped in and opened the champagne and poured them all a glass. She said, "It's a long story, but such a good one. It's about a woman who started life full of grit and toughness and ambition and energy and got so far up in her life that she forgot who she really was. And the man who loved her when she was first starting out, who saw her in a way that no one else did and loved her in a way that no one else ever had." Her eyes filled with tears. "And he waited for me." She sighed. "And then when I was in trouble I called him, and he was there for me."

She felt light-headed as she said the words, "We were married last week at City Hall in New York."

As one, the four of them cried, "But what did you wear?"

Megan O'Reilly's glance shifted nervously to her gown still hanging in its corner. She laughed, "Don't worry Megan. I didn't wear your dress. Seriously, it looks rubbish on me. I wore the very first dress I ever designed." Then, feeling girlish and proud she pulled up the photographs that Wade had forwarded. They passed her tablet computer around, admiring the photos of the wedding and a few snaps of her short honeymoon. "You look so happy," Kate said.

"I am."

She put down her glass. "You know, it's funny how the thing that you think is the worst that could possibly happen turns out to be the best? If the three of you hadn't rejected my poor dress and I hadn't truly begun to believe that I was cursed, my business was cursed and the dress was cursed, Wade and I would not be married today. You just never know in life."

Kate nodded. "That dress changed all of our destinies."

"And here's the crazy part. They found the seamstress that screamed at us, Kate. She's not a Gypsy at all. And she claims she doesn't know any curses. She was only attempting to upset me."

"She seemed completely scary," Kate said with a shudder.

"I told you," Megan said, not without pride. "Didn't I tell you all? That dress isn't cursed. It's magic, in a good way."

She laid out her sketches for bridesmaid dresses. "For each of you, I have designed a slightly different style with the same basic theme. Naturally, since all of us are now married except for Megan, we'll all be matrons of honor. But who cares about that. I've got fabric samples here. I think we should go with one fabric and four slightly different dress designs. She handed each woman a pencil sketch of her and her dress and had the pleasure of seeing each of them fall in love. She had such a clear vision of all of them and when she saw their faces she knew she had got it right. Exactly right.

Megan, of course, did not have a bridesmaid dress of her own and she was the one who saw what she'd done. She said, "They all have a similar design to my wedding dress."

Gabby nodded. "Exactly. I've designed it as an organic whole. The dresses are similar but different. What do you think?"

Megan stood up and spun in a circle. "I love it so much I can't even believe it. When I walked down Melrose and saw that dress in the window of Joe's Past and Present I never could have believed a fairy tale groom and a fairy tale dress would come together for my fairy tale wedding. It's going to be a beautiful ceremony."

"You should seriously think about branching out into bridesmaid dresses," Tasmine said. Tasmine, Gabby recalled, was in sales and understood about expanding product lines.

Once more she nodded enthusiastically. "That's exactly what I'm going to do." She was bubbling with excitement and enthusiasm and new ideas.

She felt somehow, as mysterious and hokey as it sounded, that when she had fallen in love with Wade all over again, she'd come to realize that Evangeline had taken away too much of Gabby. Gabby needed to reassert herself and when she did, she became the most creative she'd ever been in her whole life. She said, "I am going to begin designing bridesmaid dresses. In fact, I'm starting a whole new bridal line. I want to make my gowns accessible to everyone. I don't want a girl like you, Megan, to walk past a store and feel like she can't afford my gowns. I'll still keep designing high-end bridal couture for private clients, but I've decided to expand my business with a line of much more affordable prêt-à-porter formalwear."

"That's fantastic," Tasmine said.

Kate had a tiny frown between her eyebrows. She said, "Will

you still have a policy of only designing for attractive women?" Kate, she recalled, worked with teenage girls at risk. She shook her head, ashamed of some of her practices. Former practices, she reminded herself.

"When I came out of the wedding ceremony last week, there were all these brides and grooms waiting to get married and every one of those women was beautiful. They were all shapes and sizes and I realized what a snob I'd been."

She sighed, "From now on, Evangeline is an all-sizes bridal boutique."

CHAPTER 18

$\mathcal{E}$vangeline had always said that every woman should have a perfect wedding dress. And, that had never been truer than today.

She stood in the back of the tiny church. This was her first time as a bridesmaid and she was quite determined to do a very good job. The four bridesmaids all wore variations of gowns in a deep turquoise silk that flattered every one of them.

For all the trouble Megan's dress had caused her, now that the moment was finally here she realized that the infamous gown on this particular bride was stunning. If she did say so herself, that gown, with these bridesmaid dresses, was going to be one of her proudest achievements.

She adjusted the shoulders of the dress ever so slightly on Megan O'Reilly's shoulders. Then she stepped back. "You are a beautiful bride." The other three bridesmaids all nodded in agreement. Ashley, always the most outspoken one, said, "I know. It's so weird, how that dress never really looked right on any of us and when you wear it it's like it was meant to be."

Evangeline didn't argue with her. She still thought the dress had looked pretty good on Kate, but nothing compared to what it looked like on Megan. She said, "And to think I actually believed that the dress was cursed."

Kate and Ashley exchanged glances. Kate said, "To be honest with you, after that woman screamed at you, I thought it was cursed too."

It was Megan who shook her head, so her elegant, sexy curls wobbled. "No. I never felt that." She looked at Gabby with the same look of appeal she'd given her when she was begging for the dress. "I knew, the second I stepped into it, something happened. I don't believe in curses, anyway." She grinned at all of them. "But I do believe in magic."

Gabby nodded slowly. "You know, you're right. The dress never did anything bad. In fact, it prevented all of you from marrying the wrong people. The dress introduced Megan to Dylan and brought Wade and me back together. She patted both Megan and the dress lightly. "For as much trouble as it's caused, this gown is one of the best things I've ever done."

Megan's father joined them in the back room of the church. He rubbed his hands. Gabby could see where his daughter got the red hair from. He was proud and slightly conspicuous in his brand-new navy suit. He said, "Well girls? Are you ready?"

Megan sighed in bliss. "I've never been more ready for anything."

As much as the bridesmaids might have liked to be paired with their own men, Dylan, of course, had his own friends.

Kate went first. Before she set off down the aisle, Gabby, who'd spent half her life on the catwalk, gave the women some quick pointers. "Head up. Don't look at your feet. Big smile on your face and imagine you're floating."

Kate nodded. "Thanks. I never had a walk-down-the-aisle type wedding, it's surprisingly nerve-racking."

"Smile and float. You'll be fine."

And she did. Since there was no wedding coordinator, Gabby had taken on the unofficial role of being in charge of the bridesmaids. She waited a few beats and then whispered to Ashley, "Smile and float." Ashley headed off with a lot more confidence. She could see the husbands all sitting on the bride's side of the church. Four strong, handsome men. She felt a wave of affection for all of them as each focused on his own woman as she made her way up the aisle. Tasmine went next. She didn't need any reminders about smiling. That girl had cheerleader written all over her. Her smile was big and bright and her step confident as she stepped out down the aisle. While she watched, handsome Eric Van Hoffendam blew his bridesmaid a kiss.

And then it was her turn. Like Kate, she hadn't had a formal wedding. But somehow, this was the perfect way for her to walk down the aisle. With that crazy, magic dress, but without having to wear it.

Her memories of her own wedding day were perfect. She even loved that there were no formal photographs. At the press reception they'd offered the pictures snapped on Wade's cell phone. Since she wasn't completely foolish where the media were concerned, she had also talked Wade into hiring the services of the resident photographer at their resort to snap a couple of photographs of them on their honeymoon. The media had happily used those.

She took her own advice. Taking a moment, as she had during her entire modeling career, just before she stepped out, she took a breath and centered herself. Usually, on the catwalk, the models were directed not to smile. The attention was meant to be on the clothing, so they were essentially walking mannequins, but this wasn't the catwalk and she was showing off her own designer dress. Plus, this was an occasion to celebrate. Her dress had helped make five couples very happy. What was there not to smile about? As she walked down the aisle holding her bouquet she glanced at Wade. He sent her the smile he kept just for her. When she arrived at the top of the aisle, Megan and her father were coming up behind her. She felt a lump rise in her throat—not only for Megan who was as radiant a bride as any had ever been and who floated effortlessly towards the gorgeous man standing waiting for her, but also to see her dress finally get its walk down the aisle.

Like Gabby herself, the dress had suffered a few wrong turns, a few bad matches, and had finally found its perfect mate. Just like Megan and Dylan, Kate and Nick, Ashley and Ben, Tasmine and Eric, and she and Wade.

When that woman had screamed what turned out to be the first verse of the Hungarian National Anthem at her, and claimed it was a curse, she could never have imagined that such an awful moment could lead to this perfect one.

When Dylan slipped the wedding ring onto Megan's finger and kissed her to seal the ceremony, she knew all the stress and anxiety of these crazy few months had been worth it.

The reception was held at a small French restaurant with a garden out back.

Wade came up and put his arm around her. "You looked beautiful," he said. And he leaned over and kissed her, just a casual kiss, the kind a couple share in a crowded place. Still, the feel of his lips on hers sent a shiver down to her toes. She wondered if she'd ever get used to that, and hoped she never did. This man, her husband. The one she'd almost lost through her own arrogance and misguided need to control everything, and the one who'd helped her see that Evangeline wasn't real.

Well, she *was* real, she was as real as these wedding dresses, but nobody wore a wedding dress every day. There was also the everyday person, the Gabby part of her. While most of her friends and colleagues shortened her name to Eve or Ev, Wade always called her Gabby. To her amusement, she realized that Kate, Tasmine, Ashley and Megan had also started calling her Gabby. She found she rather liked it.

Megan and Dylan hadn't wanted a formal receiving line, and before they were called away to mingle with their guests, the ten of them had a moment. A waiter walked up with a tray of champagne, and Gabby said, "Perfect timing. I want to make a toast."

Everyone took a glass but Kate who shook her head. "Can I have sparkling water?"

Normally she wouldn't think anything of it, but Kate blushed when she asked for the water.

Obviously, she wasn't the only one who'd noticed. Ashley said, "Is there anything you want to tell us?"

And Kate nodded, with a quick secret glance at Nick who beamed with pride. "We're going to have a baby."

When they'd all congratulated her and she had her water, Gabby raised her glass. "To Megan, for finally wearing my dress as it was meant to be worn and for looking so absolutely beautiful in it. And to Dylan for being her perfect mate. And I wish to toast each of you lovely bridesmaids for coming into my life and making it so much more special." She stopped for a second as her voice grew husky. "Somehow, because of that dress, we all found love. And now, we're going to have our first baby. Here's to perfect matches."

They all sipped and Wade said, "Maybe you should consider starting Evangeline maternity."

She threw back her head and laughed. "What a wonderful idea. That is exactly what I'm going to do."

I hope you enjoyed this romantic comedy series. If you enjoy cozy mysteries try *The Vampire Knitting Club* or for your next addictive romance series try *Kiss a Girl in the Rain*, book one in the *Take a Chance* series. Thanks for reading and I'd really appreciate it if you'd leave an honest review. It really helps!

A Note from Nancy

Dear Reader,

Thank you for reading *The Almost Wives Club* series. I am so grateful for all the enthusiasm this series has received.

I hope you'll consider leaving a review and please tell your friends who like contemporary romance or romantic comedies.

Review on Amazon, Goodreads or BookBub.

Join my newsletter for a free prequel to my *Vampire Knitting Club* series, *Tangles and Treasons*, the exciting tale of how the gorgeous Rafe Crosyer was turned into a vampire.

I hope to see you in my private Facebook Group. It's a lot of fun. www.facebook.com/groups/NancyWarrenKnitwits

Until next time,
Happy Reading,

Nancy

ALSO BY NANCY WARREN

The best way to keep up with new releases, sales, plus enjoy bonus content and prizes is to join Nancy's newsletter at NancyWarrenAuthor.com or join her private Facebook group www.facebook.com/groups/NancyWarrenKnitwits

The Almost Wives Club

An enchanted wedding dress is a matchmaker in this series of romantic comedies where five runaway brides find out who the best men really are!

The Almost Wives Club: Kate - Book 1

Second Hand Bride - Book 2

Bridesmaid for Hire - Book 3

The Wedding Flight - Book 4

If the Dress Fits - Book 5

The Almost Wives Club Box Set - Books 1-5

Take a Chance series

Meet the Chance family, a cobbled together family of eleven kids who are all grown up and finding their ways in life and love.

Chance Encounter - Prequel

Kiss a Girl in the Rain - Book 1

Iris in Bloom - Book 2

Blueprint for a Kiss - Book 3

Every Rose - Book 4

Love to Go - Book 5

The Sheriff's Sweet Surrender - Book 6

The Daisy Game - Book 7

Take a Chance Box Set - Prequel and Books 1-3

The Vampire Knitting Club

Paranormal Cozy Mysteries. When Lucy inherits her grandmother's knitting shop in Oxford, she discovers secrets and solves murders with the help of some special undead amateur sleuths.

Tangles and Treasons - a free prequel for Nancy's newsletter subscribers

The Vampire Knitting Club - Book 1

Stitches and Witches - Book 2

Crochet and Cauldrons - Book 3

Stockings and Spells - Book 4

Purls and Potions - Book 5

Fair Isle and Fortunes - Book 6

Lace and Lies - Book 7

Bobbles and Broomsticks - Book 8

Popcorn and Poltergeists - Book 9

Garters and Gargoyles - Book 10

Diamonds and Daggers - Book 11

Herringbones and Hexes - Book 12

Ribbing and Runes - Book 13

Cat's Paws and Curses - A Holiday Whodunnit

Vampire Knitting Club Boxed Set: Books 1-3

Vampire Knitting Club Boxed Set: Books 4-6

The Vampire Book Club

A middle aged witch gets sent to Ireland to run an unusual book shop.

Crossing the Lines - Prequel

The Vampire Book Club - Book 1

Chapter and Curse - Book 2

A Spelling Mistake - Book 3

The Great Witches Baking Show

The Great Witches Baking Show - Book 1

Baker's Coven - Book 2

A Rolling Scone - Book 3

A Bundt Instrument - Book 4

Blood, Sweat and Tiers - Book 5

Crumbs and Misdemeanors - Book 6

A Cream of Passion - Book 7

Gingerdead House - A Holiday Whodunnit

The Great Witches Baking Show Boxed Set: Books 1-3

Toni Diamond Mysteries

Toni is a successful saleswoman for Lady Bianca Cosmetics in this series of humorous cozy mysteries.

Frosted Shadow - Book 1

Ultimate Concealer - Book 2

Midnight Shimmer - Book 3

A Diamond Choker For Christmas - A Holiday Whodunnit

For a complete list of books, check out Nancy's website at NancyWarrenAuthor.com

ABOUT THE AUTHOR

Nancy Warren is the USA Today Bestselling author of more than 90 novels. She's originally from Vancouver, Canada, though she tends to wander and has lived in England, Italy and California at various times. While living in Oxford she dreamed up The Vampire Knitting Club. Favorite moments include being the answer to a crossword puzzle clue in Canada's National Post newspaper, being featured on the front page of the New York Times when her book Speed Dating launched Harlequin's NASCAR series, and being nominated three times for Romance Writers of America's RITA award. She has an MA in Creative Writing from Bath Spa University. She's an avid hiker, loves chocolate and most of all, loves to hear from readers! The best way to stay in touch is to sign up for Nancy's newsletter at NancyWarrenAuthor.com or www.facebook.com/groups/NancyWarrenKnitwits

To learn more about Nancy and her books
NancyWarrenAuthor.com